PENALTY

JACOB CHANCE

PENALTY

Cover designed by PopKitty Design
Edited by Vivian Freeman
Paperback formatted by Abby Web Design & Formatting

This book contains mature content.

DEDICATION

This book is dedicated to all the members of my reader's group,
Spoiled by Chance.
Thank you for all the support and encouragement you show me.
Whether you contribute regularly or prefer to sit back quietly, I
appreciate each one of you.

ACKNOWLEDGMENTS

Thank you to all the readers, bloggers and authors who've supported me. Whether you've purchased one of my books, shared my teasers or even just liked one of my posts; I'm grateful.

Diane Hamilton, my amazing PA, you deserve so much more than a simple thank you for the hundreds of things you do for me day in and day out. I hope you realize how grateful I am to have you guiding me through all this. I couldn't do it without you.

Thank you to my editor Vivian Freeman. You always know what my books need more or less of. You've made me a better writer by pointing out my addiction to certain words. My word search list grows with each book, lmao.

Thank you to Hawkeye's Proofreading. You always make time for my books and I know I can count on you to see all the typos I've missed even when I've read the final draft at least twenty times.

I have awesome beta readers. These ladies make time to read my rough draft when their schedules are already full. I can always count on them to tell me if they don't like something or if they think I need to add more. Thank you Viv, Laura, Dawn Nicole, Angela, Paula Dawn and Ceeri.

B.C.P.G - You guys keep me from writing more than I do and keep me from sleeping what little I can.

Why am I thanking you?

You also make me laugh, you're brutally honest and you challenge me when I need it. Most importantly, you support my love of the Pats and you like my accent.

Misty - Thank you for all you do for Chance Promotions. Your time and organization is greatly appreciated.

PROLOGUE

August

Grimacing at the sting of her long nails digging furrows into the skin on my back, I thrust my cock into her. She moans in my ear and her hands move down to grip my ass. Her legs squeeze my hips like a vise as I pound into her harder and deeper.

I'm surprised by how good a fuck she is. A lot of the time I find easy pussy is lazy pussy, but she's proving to be a nice exception. I don't even mind she's older than the women I usually screw. She's hot with her deep red hair, bright pink painted lips and a rack that won't quit.

Her pussy is starting to quiver around my cock now. Rubbing my fingers over her clit, circling around the swollen flesh, I slam my dick as hard as I can into her. She shrieks like a wild cat as she trembles through her orgasm. I pull out of her and remove the condom before stroking my cock until I release all over her flat stomach.

I never come inside easy pussy. I don't need some gold digger looking for a free ride, claiming I'm their baby's daddy. What would be even worse is actually being their baby's daddy. *Jesus.* That's why I always wrap and pull. I like to think of it as being *proactive*.

I grab some tissues off the hotel nightstand and wipe

her stomach clean. *I'm such a gentleman.* She stretches and yawns loudly as I slide my boxer briefs on.

"Where are you going, sugar?" She asks posing provocatively on her side. The scent of sex and her floral perfume are strong in the air. Stepping into my jeans, I pull them up. "I have some place else to be," I reply vaguely as I button and zip my pants.

"Are you sure I can't talk you into round two?" She traces a long red nail around her nipple.

My dick twitches at the thought of another go in her tight pussy, but I should finish unpacking my stuff. Two of my friends just moved into a new apartment off campus, with me. There's still a lot to be done before classes begin in a few more days.

"No, sorry I can't." I walk toward the door. "I gotta run. Maybe some other time sweetie." I pull the hotel suite door open and give her a quick wave before I go.

Closing the door, whistling the song *"The Stranger,"* my shoes are silent on the thick carpet of the ritzy hotel corridor as I head toward the exit. The woman I just fucked already all but forgotten.

CHAPTER ONE

BRADY

Early November

I grunt from the impact as the air expels from me when I'm tackled to the ground. The crowd loudly cheers, and I know my pass to my roommate, Nick, one of our team's wide receivers, hit its mark. The peal of a shrill whistle nearby cuts through all the sounds of celebration.

My buddy, Zeke, one of the offensive linemen, holds his hand out for me, pulling me up. He pats me on the back.

"You okay man?" he asks. "That was a hard hit and a late one."

"Yeah, I'm good," I say, picking grass out of the side of my face mask and throwing it to the ground. My body is wracked with pain, but I shake it off. There's no time to think about it; we need to win this game.

The announcement comes over the sound system calling for a penalty against the opposing team for roughing the passer. I'm glad the officials got their heads outta their asses this time. There were two other plays just like this one and they turned a blind eye both times.

Their penalty earns us an extra fifteen yards and lines us up on their ten-yard line with only thirty seconds left on the clock. We're down by three and need at least a field goal to tie it up, but we've got great field position. At first and goal we've got four downs to get in the end zone. We're going to get the touchdown; I can feel it in my gut.

My fingers tingle as I wait for the ball to be snapped to me. This happens to me in high pressure situations such as this one. The sound of the crowd gets drowned out in my head, my focus is complete. I get tunnel vision. Some people call it the eye of the tiger, others call it the killer instinct. I think both of those terms are too dramatic for what it really is. I'm simply good under pressure. I make shit happen on the field when it needs to. I'm a playmaker.

The ball is snapped to me. I take two steps back, and roll around to the right to avoid being sacked. My eyes scan the end zone for Nick before I draw my arm back and release the ball. It's right on target, and he catches it smoothly, holding it tightly in his grasp, before spiking it in the end zone. I run over to him, and we bump chests. The crowd erupts shouting, "touchdown."

"Fucking A, Brady. That's how it's done," Nick shouts.

"Yeah my arm makes you look better than you really are." He laughs and I whack him on the back. The rest of our teammates on the field surround us, celebrating our win. The cheers of the crowd are deafening. This victory tastes even sweeter than most. We just beat our biggest rivals.

"Jesus, could they invite some more fucking people?" I ask my buddy Zeke when another person bumps into me. The room is full of college students, and even with my excessive size, I'm having difficulty navigating through.

Being surrounded by people like this isn't something I'm comfortable with; it pisses me off. I know there's a scowl on my face, but I don't really care. I love a party just as much as the rest of the guys, but right now I just want to enjoy my beer in peace and quiet.

One of the drawbacks of no longer living in this frat house is that I can't escape to my room whenever I need a break or when I want to enjoy some alone time with whichever lucky lady I choose that night.

"Hey man, I'm gonna step outside for some fresh air. This crowd is too much for me." I run my hand through my short blonde hair.

Zeke smiles. "Yeah, I can tell. You have your mean mug on. You're going to scare all the ladies away with that face."

I smirk and point at my chiseled jawline. "The ladies love this face no matter what expression's on it."

He laughs and holds his fist out. I bump it with mine. "True story, Linc." Zeke always calls me by my nickname, short for my last name Lincoln. For as long as I can remember it's been that way. The ladies call me "The Missing Link," in reference to my bedroom skills. They say my dick is what their pussies have been missing all their lives. I think it's fucking hilarious, and I just go with it. I'm certainly not going to complain. It works in your favor when the entire female population at school thinks you're a beast between the sheets.

"I don't know why they all love you so much when you're such an asshole, but it works for you," he says. Taking a gulp of his drink, the red solo cup covers his face.

"I keep telling you women don't want to be treated well. They don't appreciate it. They all want an asshole - a bad boy and I'm more than happy to be that for them. I get pussy whenever I need and I don't bother with the hearts and fucking flowers bullshit they don't really want anyway. It's a win-win for everyone involved." I poke him in his chest. "One of these days you'll drop the good guy act and lose that clingy girlfriend of yours. Then you'll realize what you're missing out on. It's inevitable. You're only twenty-one, man, no one should settle down at such a young age."

Zeke playfully shoves me back away from him. "Dude, you're such a dickhead when it comes to women. Someday you'll meet a girl who'll knock you on your ass and you won't even know what hit you." He smiles. "I can't fucking wait."

I shove his chest. "Fuck off with your bullshit. It's never going to happen. I'm never going to have a ball and chain around my ankle. I prefer wet lips wrapped around my dick." I wink at him and he fist bumps me.

"I'll give you that. Lips around the ole shaft is where it's at, but it's even better when it's the same pair all the time."

"Sure, dude. Keep convincing yourself." I pat him on his thick chest and walk toward the kitchen for a refill.

Laughter draws my eyes to the round table in the corner of the room where a few people are playing poker. Grabbing a red cup, I fill it with fresh ice from the freezer. Chucking my empty beer bottle in the recycling bin, my eyes scan all the liquor lined up in no identifiable order on the counter. *What am I in the mood for?* I spot a bottle of Jack Daniels on the far left and pour some over the ice. The frozen cubes crack when the room temperature liquid makes contact, and my mouth waters as I anticipate taking the first sip. I add some coke and then give it a stir with a straw I found on the counter. Dropping the straw on the granite, I tip the cup back and take the first sip of the cool mixture. *Ahh, just what I needed.* This is perfect - less people and a stiff drink.

I move toward the back exit, already looking forward to relaxing on the large deck, which spans the width of the house. It was one of my favorite places to hang out when I lived here. There's a hammock in the back yard tied between two towering oaks that's calling my name. I spent many drunken nights sleeping out there. My hand is barely on the knob when the door flies open and someone crashes into me, spilling their cold drink all over the front of my shirt.

"You've got to be fucking kidding me," I snap. The gray cotton clings to me now, soaked with beer. The pungent scent is powerful and all I can smell. I step back inside the kitchen and search for a towel.

"I'm sorry," a breathless female voice answers.

"Ever heard of watching where you're going?" Scowling, I pull the soaked material away from my skin before grabbing the white dish towel hanging on the handle of the cabinet and rubbing the large stain.

"It was an accident. I didn't expect you to be there when I opened the door. You startled me." Her voice is soft and has a husky quality I find extremely sexy.

Throwing the towel down on the counter, I turn around to see if the face and body match the hot tones of her voice. Once my eyes land on the girl standing in front of me, nothing else registers. She's unbelievably gorgeous and...tiny. The top of her head only reaches my chest. Her eyes are the dark gray of a stormy sky and they're large for her small face - almost too large as she stares up at me. Waves of dark chocolate fall around her petite frame in long, loose curls. When she tucks one side behind her ear some of the strands drape over the top of her tits. I'm tempted to wind the long tresses around my fingers and reel her in for a kiss.

Her wide eyes meet mine as she nervously bites on her bottom lip. I want to know what her full pink lips would feel like pressed against mine. What would they feel like opening beneath mine letting my tongue inside to taste her?

What the fuck is this bullshit?

I don't wax poetic about some chicks looks. If she's got a banging body, then I bang her - end of story. It never goes any further. I'm not one to pay attention to what color her eyes are or notice her skin is fair and clear. I don't wonder if her cheeks would flush pink when I make her come for the first time.

Why am I'm having these thoughts about some random chick?

"What's your name, honey?" I ask, moving closer, my gaze roaming over her. She reminds me of an anime character all wide eyes, wild hair and a sexy little pout for a mouth. Jesus. Right now, just looking at her is giving me a fucking semi.

"Harlow." It's only one word, but it sends shivers down my spine like long nails scratching the length of my back.

I lean in. "Well, Harlow, now that you got my shirt all wet, what do you say I return the favor and get you wet. Soaked. And I'm not talking about your shirt." I wink at her and wait for the smile to appear on her face. The one that says I know what you really want and I want it too. Let's go fuck like rabbits on crack.

That's not the reaction I get from Harlow though. Her eyebrows move toward the middle of her forehead. Like a defensive kitten, she arches her upper body as far away from me as she can without actually taking a step. Her ability to balance while leaning so far back is impressive. And cute. A cute, angry kitten.

"I came here with friends. I can't just leave them."

I run the back of my index finger down her cheek. "Okay, kitten. We can go find them and tell them you're coming with me."

She shakes her head, frowning. "I don't even know you."

I place my hands on the countertop on either side of her, caging her in. "Are you sure about that, kitten? Everyone knows who I am. I'm the quarterback for the Terriers."

She avoids my gaze and crosses her arms in front of her. My eyes wander down to stare at the deep fuckable valley between her tits. I want my cock there. Soon.

"Stop calling me kitten. I don't really follow football." Her words draw my eyes back to her face.

"I guess it's time you started then." I tip her chin up with my fingers and flash my most irresistible smile.

She doesn't smile back. She actually looks annoyed. "I don't like football or football players. Sorry I spilled my drink on you, but I'm not going to make up for your shirt getting a little wet by blowing you back at your apartment," she huffs.

"Who said anything about you blowing me? I was thinking more along the lines of fucking you all night long."

"Okay this conversation is over. I need to go find my friends." She pushes firmly on my chest, and as much as I want to resist and keep her here with me, I don't. I take a step back so she can pass by.

I call out to her. "My name's Brady Lincoln in case you change your mind. I'm not hard to find."

I watch her curvy little ass sway with each step until she's out of sight. *Damn.* She's got some banging curves on her and a fresh little mouth I'd like to keep permanently occupied. I adjust my dick and knock the rest of my drink back.

Harlow. I like that name. It suits her. I wonder what her last name is? I'm a dumbass for not asking, but she took me by surprise. She knocked me off balance a little and girls never do. I'm not sure I like the unexpected effect she had on me, but I'm definitely intrigued by her hot curves and her spitfire mouth.

I make myself another drink and then head back to the large living room to seek her out. I want to know her last name and where she lives. I've never seen her on campus and I'm sure I'd remember if I had. She's not someone I'd forget. She's a tempting little package I can't wait to open.

My eyes scan around the crowded space for her, but I don't spot her anywhere. Leaning my back against the wall, I sip on my drink, disappointed. I was looking forward to talking with her some more. I'm sure I could've convinced her to come home with me if I had a few more minutes to lay some of the Lincoln charm on her. *Better luck next time.*

CHAPTER TWO

HARLOW

Did Brady Lincoln, the Brady Lincoln, Mr. Tom Brady Has Nothing On Me In The Looks Department, really ask me to have sex with him? I couldn't get out of that frat party fast enough. Especially after spilling my drink on Brady Lincoln. *Oh God, I still can't believe I spilled my drink on him.*

I may have acted as if I didn't know who he was, but I don't think there's a female on campus who doesn't know of him. He's the quarterback of our football team and he's rumored to be good enough to make it to the NFL.

He's way out of my league.

I've admired him from afar since the first time I saw him over a year ago. He made enough of an impression on me that I still remember the exact moment. I caught sight of him across the food court surrounded by an enamored group of hot girls. Seeing him across a crowded room sounds so cliché, but is exactly what happened. He was impossible to miss with his tall frame and broad shoulders. His gorgeous looks made my stomach flutter.

That particular day he had on a pair of low hanging jeans and a black fitted t-shirt. His muscular arms were bulging with every motion he made as he gestured with his hands explaining something to the group of giggling girls around him. I remember covertly studying him from the table I was seated at and wondering what it would be like to kiss him or to be held in those strong arms. I didn't let myself daydream about it for long, though. I'm not some girl with her head in the clouds. I'm all about the hard truths of reality. Life has dealt me its fair share of difficulties and I'm not about to moon over some egomaniac baller.

Now, over a year later, I find him even more attractive and I know for sure he's no one I want to be involved with. He's a player - he's a professional player. I can't deny there's something I find undeniably attractive about him and I can't put my finger on what it is. All I can say is once you get a look at his face you can say goodbye to your heart because his dimple laden smile will steal it right from you - even when it's directed at another girl. And all the smiles of his I've seen have always been directed at other girls - until tonight. When he flashed his flirtatious grin at me I had to fight the urge to smile back at him. When he asked me if I wanted to go back to his apartment it was all I could do to refuse him. Every part of my body wanted me to say yes - except my overworked brain. I can never get that sucker to shut down. Geez. Is it too much to ask for one night of risky behavior? I'd like one time where I don't think everything through and allow myself to cut loose and have fun.

What's it like to enjoy yourself and not worry about repercussions - to live in the moment and enjoy every second? I'll probably never know because I'm too much of a control freak to ever let that happen. I plan everything out and spontaneous isn't a word ever used to describe me. I'm responsible, predictable - *boring.* I wasn't always this way, but fate has a way of changing who we are. All we can do is make the most of the ride we're on and adapt with every sharp curve we unexpectedly travel.

Going to the party tonight was a big step for me, and my roommate Raine had to practically drag me there. As it was I left early. I couldn't stay any longer.

Brady Lincoln is a hard to resist temptation and that scares me. Someone like him could destroy my orderly little world. He makes me feel things I don't want to which worries me. I had to leave the party before I could go back in the kitchen to tell him I'd had a change of heart. I was afraid I'd beg him to take me to his apartment and then I'd let him do whatever nefarious things his wicked mind could think of. And I'm sure he can think of plenty. Even with my lack of savvy with guys I can think of a few things I'd like him to do to me.

I'm pretty sure Rob my high school boyfriend didn't know what he was doing when we had sex. He couldn't find my G-spot if his life depended on it. He couldn't even manage to locate my clit and it's not even hard to find. Still I'm not ignorant about how sex should be. I read books - a lot of books - hot books. I've got multiple book boyfriends and they can get me off way better than Rob ever could.

He never did get me off.

All my orgasms so far have been self-induced. I'm pretty good at one handed reading, but it would be nice to know what it's like to have a guy touch me the way my book boyfriends touch their women. I want to know what it's like for someone to take charge in bed and not fumble around trying to figure out what comes next.

I bet Brady doesn't know the meaning of the word fumble unless it's used in the context of football. I'm sure he's all smooth moves and confidence. I bet he'd make me feel more pleasure than I can imagine, but at the same time I also know he'd have the power to cause me more pain than my heart can take. I'm not the kind of girl who can sleep with someone once and then be cast aside. I know that's how he operates.

I need to keep my distance.

Monday sneaks up on me and I don't want to go to class this morning. All I want to do is climb back in my bed and fall into a deep slumber. I didn't sleep well last night. Thoughts of Brady Lincoln had my head spinning. I hate that I don't even know him and he has this weird power over me. He can completely consume my thoughts even though we didn't even engage in some lengthy conversation. Our total interaction amounted to under five minutes, but it was the most exhilarating five minutes of my life. I don't know if my heart has ever pounded so hard unless I was exercising.

Somehow, I manage to make it through my first class without falling asleep, and now I've a break for over an hour. I head toward the cafe down the street from school, my mouth already watering at the thought of the large muffins they sell.

When I walk inside my nose is assaulted with the scent of fresh baked goods combined with coffee. I pause for a moment, close my eyes and inhale. I love this place so much I've been toying with the idea of getting a job here since I started my freshman year; even though I don't have to work. I'm fortunate my stepmom Cindy has the financial means to pay for my schooling.

My dad was killed in a car accident when I was sixteen years old. I was with him and we were hit by another vehicle. It came out of nowhere and disappeared just as quickly like a thief in the night. And I guess thief would be an accurate description. After all, whoever hit us did steal my father from me - my forty year old father who had way more life left in him.

They never caught the person who was driving or found the vehicle that hit us. Everything happened so fast I didn't even see what the other car looked like and there were no witnesses.

Me - *I'm going to the store with my dad.*

I text my friend Samantha from the passenger seat of my dad's car. My father is a creature of habit and every Friday night he goes to the store at this time like clockwork. This time I decided to keep him company.

Sam - *Can you sleep over tonight?*

"Dad, can you drop me off at Sam's? Can I stay over?" I glance over at him, waiting for his answer.

He smiles. "I don't see a problem with that."

Dropping my head down, I begin to type out a reply to Sam when our car is slammed into. The crunch of metal is so loud in my ears and the impact of the crash rocks us with so much force I bounce around even with my seat belt holding tight across my chest and my lap. My cellphone flies out of my hands and my fingers drop to clutch each side of my leather seat, holding on for dear life.

"Daddy, what's happening?" I scream.

My dad loses control of the car, the steering wheel jerks from side to side in his hands as he tries to regain control.

"Hang on," he shouts, never taking his eyes off the icy winter road. We begin to slide, the tires unable to find any traction on the treacherous surface. Time slows, every second dragging out. The tires hit the edge of the median and our car goes airborne. It seems like we're flying through the air for minutes instead of merely a second or two. The vehicle lands on the driver's side with a horrifying crunch and then flips over onto the roof with another ear deafening crack. The eerie screech of metal sliding on the pavement assaults my ears making an already terrifying situation even more so as we continue to move. I've never heard anything like this cacophony of sounds and I know I'll never forget it for as long as I live. If I survive this.

The first few months that followed left me fearful of going to sleep. Each night I would relive it all over again. Even though I still hear all the sounds as well as see them in my nightmares, I can go months without dreaming about it at all.

The EMT's lost my father en route to the hospital and they were never able to revive him. Miraculously, I walked away almost completely unscathed - physically anyway. I needed sixteen stitches in my forehead along my hairline. *One for every year I had with my dad.* Mentally, I know I'll never be the same. Devastation like I'd never imagined became a part of my daily existence. It had always been dad and me. And suddenly I was alone.

Cindy never discusses the details with me, but I know my dad's life insurance policy was large. He used to jokingly say if anything happened to him she'd be set to live the rest of her life with some boy toy. He'd kid that she should be the first suspect if he suddenly disappeared.

While I haven't seen her with any younger men, we do live comfortably, but not extravagantly. Of course, the reminder of where the money came from is never easy. She's not great about communicating with me in general, never mind about details she doesn't want to share. I don't need to know how much money she received, I'd prefer some positive attention from her. I wish our relationship was different. She's been my stepmother for as long as I can remember and I love her, but we've never been close. My dad and she were married when I was only a year old. My own mother signed her rights away as soon as I was born. She wanted nothing to do with being a mother and my dad couldn't convince her otherwise.

Cindy has always been cold toward me, but at least she didn't walk away. Things have gotten more strained between us and without my father as a buffer it's more noticeable. I was my dad's girl and losing him left a huge void. My own mother didn't want me and I lost the one person who loved me unconditionally. If it wasn't for school, I'm sure I would've gotten lost in the loneliness I sometimes feel. I use college as a means to fill an empty space inside me. Raine, my classes, studying - they all help me cope.

Paying for my coffee and muffin, I settle at a table near the large front windows to people watch. This cafe is on Commonwealth Avenue, right near Boston University. It's a busy area and there's a wide variety of people shuffling along the sidewalk – men and women in business attire, and students with bleary eyes from lack of sleep. And then there's Will – or at least that's what I call him. I don't know his story, but I know he 'will work for food,' and he'll do what's necessary to survive. He's on this corner every day like clockwork, his sign and cup in hand. I wonder what his story is? How did he get to this point in his life?

Are we all balancing on a fine invisible wire and the slightest thing can knock us off and send our lives into a tailspin?

After my father died it sure felt as if that were the case. Now, I try to make the most of each day, but I know I need to enjoy life more. I should stop holding back. It's what my dad would want for me.

Resting my elbows on the small table, I cup my chin between my palms. I like to watch the couples as they walk past holding hands. Are they whispering secrets to each other or endearments meant only for them?

An older couple walks by and my eyes follow them. They're holding hands and the woman leans into him, gazing up with a smile on her lips. She looks so in love, so completely enamored.

What's it like to be with someone for as long as I imagine they've been? What would it be like to be so in sync with someone – to know what they're going to say before they even form the words – to anticipate their every need so they might never want for anything?

I want that someday.

I want to know what it's like to connect with someone on the deepest level. I want the kind of love not everyone gets to experience.

My daddy always told me I was one of a kind and that was a good thing. I remind myself of his words whenever I feel like a square peg trying to fit inside a round hole.

The rest of the week passes quickly by, but my professors have certainly piled on the workload. Getting good grades is important to me, I study during most of my free time.

My obsessive exam preparation drives Raine crazy. She tells me I'm going to ruin my eyesight with all the reading I've been doing.

"Come on. This is ridiculous." Raine throws her hands up in the air. "Get ready, we're going out."

I look up from the psychology notes I'm studying and blow my long bangs out of my eyes. "Do I look like I want to go out tonight?" I gesture at my grease stained t-shirt and flannel pajama bottoms.

She walks over and slams my laptop closed. "We're going out. You've been holed up in this room for days now. The only time you leave is to go to class." She shakes her head and looks at me with disapproval. "It's not healthy to just study. You need a life outside of academia, Harlow."

I know she means well, but life is so much simpler when I just focus on school and nothing else. Ever since last weekend when I met Brady I've been on edge. Everywhere I go I wonder if I'll see him and when I don't I'm disappointed. It's gotten so bad my eyes scan the campus for his broad shoulders and blonde hair. They carefully peruse crowds looking for his sky blue eyes and toothpaste ad perfect smile. It's pathetic, and I hate myself a little for it.

"Why would you do that?" I cross my arm over my chest. "I was in the middle of something important." I narrow my eyes at her annoyed she touched my computer.

She glares at me, her hands on her hips. "You think everything is important. What could be more important than your own sanity? You're a psychology major for God's sake. You know how important it is to find a balance between hard work and fun." She frowns at me. "This is not balance." She curls her upper lip and looks me over, before gesturing at me. "This is a hot mess." She snorts and starts to laugh.

Giggling, I throw my pen at her and watch her bat it away. She's right. I am a mess. I'll give her that. Maybe a break from all this studying would do me some good. "Okay we can go out, but I'm not going to any frat parties," I warn her. I'm trying to avoid Brady Lincoln, not that he'd pay me the time of day if we saw each other. I'm more worried about my lack of control. I might throw myself at his feet and beg him to have his wicked way with me.

An hour later we're about to enter one of the most popular bars near campus. I've been properly dressed up by Raine. She said I look hot, but I feel like I look ridiculous. I'm wearing my tightest pair of jeans and a black fitted long sleeve shirt she picked out of her closet. The neckline is low and the tops of my boobs are hanging out for anyone to see. Geez. I need to remember not to bend over at any point. She wanted me to wear heels, but I threw my red converse on while she was in the bathroom and by the time she noticed we were already halfway to Flynn's Pub.

I don't wear heels. I'm uncoordinated. Adding heels to the mix is just asking for trouble. The frat party is the perfect example. I spilled my drink all over Brady for no apparent reason. He didn't bump into me, he just startled me a little and *bam* – he's covered in beer.

I hand my fake license over to the bouncer checking them at the door without a care in the world. This one looks legit and it never gets questioned. My ex Rob couldn't give me an orgasm, but he did manage to get me an incredible fake i.d. which makes the less than stellar year we spent together worth it.

Once we're inside, I pause and glance around. There are so many people jammed into this place. I'm not even sure how to make my way to the bar.

Raine notices my hesitation and grabs my hand. "Come on." She gives me a tug, and I follow along. She doesn't let go of my hand, and we somehow remain connected even though we're getting banged around like the small metal ball in a game of pinball.

My head swivels around when I feel a hand slide across the bottom of my ass. "Hey," I shout at the guy walking behind me. He holds his hands up like he didn't do anything, but the laughter erupting from his friends tells me different.

"Don't be an asshole." I scowl at him.

Raine keeps moving, pulling me along, and he has the audacity to wink at me.

Who does he think he is?

Just because he's hot doesn't mean he has the right to act like a dickhead. Stuff like this makes me prefer to hermit in my dorm room.

Why did I come out again tonight?

"I'm ordering shots for us. You need to get some alcohol in you. Loosen up, girl."

I huff and cross my arms over my chest. "That jerk back there felt me up." I gesture in his direction with my head.

"That jerk happens to be Cameron Davis our football team's starting running back. He can do whatever he wants to me," she jokes. "He's so hot. I've heard he's a stud between the sheets, too." She casts a coy glance in his direction with her green eyes and twirls her long blonde hair. "I wouldn't mind going home with him tonight."

What? "Raine, how gross. He's an asshole." I glance in Cameron's direction and find him smirking at me. I narrow my eyes before looking back at Raine. "He just felt my ass up, and you want to go home with him anyway? What the hell? Where's the loyalty?"

"Don't be so dramatic, Harlow. He touched your ass – so what? Don't make a big deal out of nothing." She shakes her head at me before walking up to the bar to place an order.

Rubbing my forehead with my palm, I wonder if I should just go home. This night has been a disaster so far.

"Here, drink up. You'll feel better once you've had a couple." She hands me a shot glass.

"What is this?" I hold it up to my nose and sniff.

"It's Patron. You'll like it. What should we drink to?"

Going home?

Closing my eyes for a moment, I take a deep breath. I need to quit being so negative and give this a go. Raine's always good about being there for me and I don't want to ruin her night out. Smiling at her, I decide to make the most of the situation. "Here's to you, here's to me, the best of friends we'll always be; but if we ever disagree, fuck you, here's to me." I clink my glass against hers. She giggles and we both tip them back in one strong gulp. I must admit, it tastes pretty damn good.

"Here, I ordered two for each of us," she mentions, handing me another glass.

I hold it up my eyes, staring at the liquor. "Here's to those who wish us well and those who don't can go to hell."

Raine snorts, then touches her glass to mine. We both drink them back and smile at each other. I'm starting to have some fun now.

A large hand clamps down on my shoulder, and when I swing my head around, the smile fades. *Brady Lincoln.*

"What's the matter, Harlow? If I didn't know better, I'd think you weren't happy to see me." He smiles and every coherent thought in my brain is gone. I can't believe I've been struck dumb by a jock.

What's wrong with me? I'm surprised he remembers my name. Then again, I'm probably the first girl who's ever turned him down.

His eyes are so beautiful, I get distracted staring at them. They're mesmerizing, and when I finally snap my own away, I notice his lips are curved into a knowing smirk.

I compose myself enough to answer him. "Nothing's wrong. We're just doing shots." His hand slides down to cup my upper arm in his warm palm. Just that simple touch has my body reacting. My heart is racing and my legs are trembling.

"What are you ladies drinking?" I open my mouth to tell him we don't need anyone to buy us shots when Raine interrupts.

"Patron, thanks." She smiles at me when I flash her a death glare. I don't want Brady to stick around. Now he's buying us drinks and I'm going to need to play nice with him. I move my arm to loosen his hold, but instead of letting me go like I anticipated, he slides his hand down, taking mine.

Oh, my God. I can't believe I'm holding hands with Brady Lincoln.

I glance down to make sure I'm not imagining this. Nope, I'm not and his smooth palm is hot against mine. My mind conjures up visions of me lying on his bed while those large hands slowly slide all over my stomach, pushing my shirt with them.

"Here you go, kitten," Brady's voice snaps me out of my unwanted fantasies. Glancing up at him, I find him smiling down at me. My face flushes. Crap. I grab the glass and down the shot. I squeeze my eyes shut. Cocky Brady is hard to resist, but sweet Brady might be my undoing.

What is he doing flirting with someone like me?

I open my eyes and find him studying me. His stare is too much and I lower my chin before looking in the other direction.

He hands Raine a shot. "Thanks Brady,"

"Harlow." I hear his voice but I stubbornly remain facing away from him. "Harlow." This time his voice is close to my ear and it surprises me. I shiver, liking the way his warm breath feels on my skin – *liking it too much.*

I tug on my hand, but he won't let go. When my head whips around to tell him off, my long bangs fall in my eyes. I reach up with my free hand to push them back, but he beats me to it. Gently pushing them to the side with his fingertips, he tucks them behind my ear.

Pensively biting on my bottom lip, I stare up at him.

Who is this guy?

One minute he's a cocky asshole and the next he's unbelievably sweet. He has me completely off balance and I don't know what to make of him.

Which one is the real Brady?

.

CHAPTER THREE

BRADY

God this girl – she gets to me. I don't know what it is about her, but I'm torn between wanting to hold her in my arms and wanting to bury my cock inside her for the next week straight. Her big gray eyes are so expressive. I can see everything in them, all the things she'd rather keep to herself. She's afraid of her attraction to me. I usually snap my fingers and they follow. She's the first one I've met who's shown any resistance to my charm. I can see her balancing on the edge, but I'm not sure which way she'll decide to go. I think she's going to need a little push.

I flag down Jodie the bartender and she saunters over with a smile on her red, glossy lips. I'm familiar with her lips and what they're capable of. She's given me head more than once. She sucks dick like a pro and swallows every drop like a champ. Looking at her now I feel nothing. I used her to get off. I know I'm an asshole for it, but at least she knew what she was getting. Making promises to the women I screw around with, isn't something I ever do.

"What can I get you handsome?" she asks.

"Three shots of Patron." She winks at me and I look down at Harlow standing next to me. Thankfully, she's not paying attention to Jodie's flirtatious behavior. I know that would just be one more reason she'd use to convince herself to stay away from me.

Jodie places the shots down and sends one more heated look my way, but I'm not biting. Placing a few bills on the bar, I slide Raine's shot toward her. She raises it when I turn to hand Harlow hers.

"Harlow and I always do a toast whenever we drink shots. It's just a little rule of ours. She comes up with some good ones," she explains. "What are we toasting to Harlow?" Raine asks.

I pick up my drink and wait while my eyes shift to Harlow. She chews on her bottom lip and stares down into her shot glass.

"Everyone should believe in something. I believe I'll have another drink." She giggles, clinks her glass against mine and then Raine's.

God, she's adorable. I'm totally enamored with this girl. Knocking the shot back, I slide the empty glass along the bar. Glancing around, I notice some of my teammates across the room. Cameron Davis is looking at Harlow. His stare has a predatory quality to it and I don't fucking like it, but I can't say I really like Cam either. He's the starting running back on our team and he's immensely talented. He's also a giant egomaniac asshole. He and I aren't friends. I tolerate him only for the sake of the team.

Releasing Harlow's hand, I proprietarily place my palm on her lower back, staking my claim. I want him to know she's off limits.

Her head tips up at me questioningly, gray eyes wide and filled with uncertainty, her mouth still glossy from the shot. It's all I can do to keep myself from stealing an unexpected kiss from her. The urge to taste her lips is so strong it takes every ounce of resolve in me to hold back. I want to show her how combustible we'll be together, but I don't want our first kiss to be in a bar. Instead, I lean down and kiss the top of her head. She tenses up. The silky strands are soft on my lips and cling to them as I pull away. It's not the kiss I'm craving, but it'll have to do for now.

"Relax," I coax and let my hand stroke down over the long, shiny length of her hair.

"Here guys." Raine appears with six more shots. We each take one in hand.

"It's better to spend tonight like there's no tomorrow, than to spend tonight like there's no money," Harlow says not missing a beat. We all touch our glasses to murmurs of "here, here," and then tip the shots back.

I slam my glass down on the bar upside down and notice Jodie's eyes on me.

"Okay, one more for now," Raine draws my attention as she hands us our glasses. She looks at Harlow, waiting for her to say something. She has a small smile playing on her full lips. She looks mischievous and I can't wait to hear what's about to come out of her mouth.

Harlow lifts her glass. "The rose may kiss the butterfly, the wine may kiss the crystal glass, a girl may kiss her man goodbye, but you my friends may kiss my ass." She barely finishes the toast before laughter peals out of her. Her laugh is adorable. Christ, everything about this girl entices me. I need to convince her to give me a chance. I know if she goes on one date with me, she'll see I'm not the asshole she thinks I am. I need to have her under me – on top of me – any way I can.

Over the course of the next hour we drink a few more shots and keep the conversation light. When Cameron comes over to talk to Raine, Harlow moves over to my side, burrowing in as close as she can get. I tuck my arm around her and wonder if she has history with him.

Did he do something to her?

I don't want to ask her now and risk upsetting her. She's just starting to act like I'm not the devil and it's probably because she's drunk and her defenses are down, but I'll take what I can get.

Another hour passes and now I'm sitting on a stool leaning on the bar behind me. My eyes may be looking out at the crowd, but I'm very much focused on this sweet girl standing between my legs with her back to my chest. She's relaxed, my arms are loose around her waist. I want to pull her against me so she can feel the hard on trying to bust out of my jeans, but I don't want to scare her off. I already know she's not like other girls. She flat out turned me down and I can't treat her the same as I do them. I want nothing more than to be naked in my bed with her at this very moment. Hell, I'd settle for bending her over the bathroom sink in the men's room right now. Fuck. I really need to stop thinking about this. I know I won't be getting any relief for my blue balls between Harlow's sexy thighs.

My eyes land on a cute blonde across the room. Looking her over, I wonder if I've ever messed around with her before. She's giving me the look and I know all I'd have to do is crook my finger at her or flash her a smile and she'd be at my beck and call. It might be nice to sink my dick inside some new pussy tonight. I haven't gotten laid for almost two weeks now.

Harlow spins around in my arms and stares up at me with her wide stormy gray eyes wiping out all thoughts of any other woman. No matter how much I try to convince myself I'd bury my dick in any pussy, now that she's on my radar – *I don't want to.*

CHAPTER FOUR

HARLOW

When I open my eyes, the bright morning sunshine feels like knives repeatedly stabbing my forehead. I snap them closed and groan. Fuck.

Why'd I drink so much at the bar? Oh God. My head aches so bad. Covering my eyes with one hand, I block out the rays of sunlight coming in the window.

Is it possible to die from a hangover? If not, I might just be the first documented case. I lick my lips and notice the horrible taste in my mouth. Gross. I'd kill for some mouthwash right now, but it would be too much work to get out of bed. I think I'd prefer to stay here and succumb to my hangover. Harlow Summers hangover death patient zero. I'll be famous on all college campuses nationwide and used in public service ads as an example of how not to act like a complete newb when you've already been in college for two years.

Snuggling down under the covers, I pray I'll feel better soon. My feet are freezing and so are my legs. I must've been too drunk to put on pajama bottoms and socks. While sliding my feet back and forth on the smooth sheets to warm them, the bottom of my foot makes contact with a hairy leg. Gasping, my foot quickly retreats to my side. Another gasp escapes me when I sit up and realize who's in bed beside me – *Brady Lincoln*. Pain grips my head and my hands move up to gently cradle both sides of it.

"You..." Is all that comes out. I'm at a loss for words.

He smiles, his dimple in his right cheek showing. "Me," he says with a wink and a nod of his head. "Good morning, kitten. This isn't the reaction I usually get from women in my bed."

"How...you...me?" I sputter, clearly frazzled. As if waking up with him wasn't bad enough, I have no idea how I ended up here in his very large comfortable bed and not in my own twin sized bed. I glance down and notice I'm wearing a Boston University Terriers shirt and I know it must be his. My hands drop to smooth over the material, then pluck it away from my chest. "Did you undress me?" I question, my voice shrill.

He sits up and the sheet slips down to his lap revealing his bare chest. My mouth drops open and I can't stop my body's reaction to him no matter how hard I try. I could possibly be drooling. I don't think I've ever seen such a muscular torso in my entire life. It's all I can do to stop myself from stretching my arm out so my fingers can graze his chest. I want to trace them over the BU Terriers mascot tattooed there and then let my hand run down over the ridges of his abs.

I need to get out of here. Brady Lincoln is the ultimate bad boy treat for someone who's as sex starved as I am. He's like a piece of cake fresh from the oven, dripping with a thick layer of frosting, tempting you to stray from your diet. It tastes so good at the time, but then the self-loathing sets in because you've been trying to lose five pounds you gained during freshman year – *make that six now* and you hate yourself for being too weak to resist.

Brady Lincoln is my "cake."

He's a threat to my methodical practices and it's time for me to get the hell out of here.

"Harlow, calm down. I didn't take advantage of you while you were passed out." He runs his fingers through his messy hair pushing it back off his face. "You got really drunk and Raine was leaving with Cameron. I told her I'd make sure you got home safe. We were in the cab heading toward your place when you made the driver pull over. You got so sick, you could barely stand. I knew I couldn't leave you alone. I brought you back here because it was closer and I changed your shirt because it was a mess. But, I didn't touch your bra; you did. And don't worry I turned my back like a perfect gentleman. I didn't see a thing – or two things." He winks at me.

Oh. My. God. I threw up in front of Brady Lincoln. My face burns with embarrassment. This couldn't get much worse – unless I threw up on him. Crap.

"I didn't throw up on you, did I?" My voice is a panicked squeak.

He chuckles. "No, I managed to avoid the line of fire."

Oh, dear god. My head slumps forward. If it was possible to die from humiliation I'd be a spirit floating merrily away right now. Death might be preferable to the remorse I'm experiencing.

I slide to the edge of the bed and hold his shirt down over my ass while rising to my feet. He's seen enough of me already.

"Where are my clothes?" I question, not spotting them anywhere.

"I washed them and threw them in the dryer for you." He slides out of bed and my eyes track his every move, checking him out from head to toe, front to back and every imaginable angle in between.

My eyeballs move to his snug, black boxer briefs and the obvious morning wood he's sporting. I don't want to look at him; I'm trying not to. I know this is the only time I'll have this opportunity because I don't plan to see Brady again. *Ever.*

And like metal drawn to a magnet, my gaze can't seem to resist the pull of his almost naked body. I hope he's not paying attention.

He pulls on a clean white t-shirt and some black basketball shorts, looking like the quintessential athlete.

"Let me grab your stuff and then I'll make you some breakfast."

"No." The word leaves me with more force than I intended, but there's no way I want to stay here with him any longer than I have to. "I'm not hungry anyway," I reply, nervously tugging at the bottom of the shirt I'm wearing. I'm not used to being in this situation. I've never spent the night with a guy other than my ex-boyfriend Rob and even though Brady and I didn't even kiss, it's still unbelievably awkward.

"Okay then, no food. Gotcha. I'll just go grab your clothes for you." He gestures toward the door with his head and I nod. Sitting down on the edge of his large bed my eyes roam around his room. The walls are painted a dull white and he has BU sports memorabilia displayed on a bookcase situated between two large windows. His steel topped desk sits against one of the side walls and there's a closed laptop situated on it. The rest of the desktop is clean and clutter free. A tall dark stained bureau stands against the wall closest to where I'm seated. The wood is marked up with numerous scratches like he bought it used or maybe it came with the apartment. It doesn't seem like something the son of a former NFL player would own. I wonder what else about him would surprise me?

"Here you go," his deep voice interrupts my thoughts. I shouldn't be thinking about him at all. I need to get the hell out of here and pretend I never met Brady.

He hands me my jeans and shirt and I notice how neatly they're folded. It was considerate of him to wash them for me. This guy keeps surprising me and I don't like it – not one little bit. I don't want him to be more than the young, dumb, full of come jock I've always assumed he was.

"Thank you," my voice is soft, barely more than a whisper. He has me feeling emotionally off balance and it's completely out of character for me. I don't let people close enough to affect me like this. Even Rob my ex-boyfriend never made me feel this thrilling sense of unease.

Being around Brady is exciting and frightening at the same time. So many untapped possibilities for us to explore and so much devastation when he gets what he wants from me and casts me aside like every other girl he's slept with.

Rising to my feet, I glance up at him. An icy jolt of awareness runs through me when our eyes lock. It makes me shiver. My attraction to him is gaining momentum with each second spent in his presence. His blue eyes are hypnotic and I have to force myself to look away.

I hold my bundle of clothes in front of my chest like a shield to protect me from the heat of his gaze as he slowly looks me over from the tips of my purple toe nails to the top of my dark unruly morning hair.

A muscle tics in his cheek. "Get dressed. I'll be waiting in the kitchen." His voice is hoarse.

I nod and as soon as he's closed the door behind him I tear his t-shirt off, throwing it on the bed. Slipping my bra and shirt on, like I'm in a race against the clock, I remind myself not to think about how comfortable his t-shirt felt against my skin. I shouldn't think about how it smelled like him either.

Sliding my jeans over my hips, I scan his floor for my missing socks while zipping up and buttoning. Spotting both peeking out from under his bed, I scoop them up and sit on the edge of the mattress to tug them on my feet.

Once my shoes are on my eyes make one final journey around Brady Lincoln's private sanctuary knowing without a doubt this is the only time I'll ever be in this room.

Soon he'll tire of me turning him down. The thrill of the chase will turn into annoyance at the amount of work it's become. He'll want a girl who puts out and expects nothing in return. That will never be me.

I bet he's never had to really work for anything. It must be nice to get everything handed to you just because your dad is Lawrence Lincoln, a former NFL player, who now hosts a sports talk show on ESPN. From what I remember, he looks like an older version of Brady; still handsome even in his early fifties. He married some socialite, and they live in New York City. I'm sure Brady will follow the same path as his father which is just one more reason on an extremely long list of why I need to avoid him at all costs.

In his bathroom, I find a brush on top of the countertop and make short work of removing the knots from my morning hair. It takes some effort to get them out and when I'm done I smooth my hand over it. Looking in the mirror at my pale face and my big eyes smudged with the prior night's makeup I look like I've been on a mad bender or fucked hard.

I wish.

Stop it. I scold myself. Thinking about Brady is a big no-no. *N.O. Do not go there.*

"Do you know where my phone is?" I ask as I enter the kitchen. Brady is facing away from me, giving my eyes the opportunity to study his broad shoulders in his plain white t-shirt. His broad back tapers down to lean hips. His black shorts hang loose but I can still make out the shape of his muscular ass. I want to squeeze it and see if it's as firm as it looks. I blow my bangs out of my eyes frustrated at the direction my thoughts have once again wandered. I wonder if I'll ever be able to stop myself from thinking about him. I need a magic wand and a spell to wipe him from my mind and make all memories of him disappear. I picture a little puff of smoke leaving my head.

No more Brady in my brain.

Walking across the large kitchen, I stop next to him. He's pouring a frothy white mixture from the blender into two glasses. He slides one along the granite counter in my direction.

I glance at the beverage and then flick my eyes to him. "What is that?" I curl my upper lip in distaste.

He smiles at me, raises his glass to his mouth and swallows the drink down in one large gulp. "Ahh." He licks his manly lips and my eyes follow the path of his tongue. I never wanted to be a tongue so badly.

"Are you going to try it?" He smirks at me and I know he just busted me fantasizing about his tongue. I'm sure his tongue is very dexterous.

Crap, here I go again thinking about him.

Maybe I need a lobotomy. They can surgically remove the piece of my brain he's lodged in.

"What is it?" I skeptically ask. Just based on what it looks like, I don't think it can possibly taste good.

"Just try it. Come on, be daring." His eyes appear a lighter shade of blue in the bright morning sunlight as they sparkle mischievously at me.

I shake my head. "No way. Not until I know what it's made of. I prefer to be safe." I hope he understands what my words mean. I'm not the kind of girl he wants. He doesn't want orderly and predictable, he wants someone who's going to leap first and look later.

That will never be me.

"Sometimes you just need to try something new – push yourself out of your comfort zone." He stares down into my eyes and rakes his teeth over his bottom lip.

Is he trying to tell me something? I suck at this reading between the lines thing. *I need an interpreter for this shit.*

I sweep my bangs off my forehead and look away. Flirting is a fine art I've never had time or the desire to develop, but right now in this moment I'm kicking myself for it. I wish I knew what to say to him. Instead, I'm paralyzed by feelings of inadequacy which only makes me seem more awkward.

He inches the glass closer to me with his fingertips. I notice how large his hands are and his nails are clipped short. I wonder what they'd feel like on my skin? On the inside of my thighs?

Oh fuck. I grab the ice-cold beverage and tip it back, swallowing down the first taste. Anything to get my mind off his hands tracing along my skin.

Dear God, make it stop.

I gulp down the rest of the vanilla tasting mixture and slam my glass down on the countertop. I cover my lips with my hand as my taste buds get hit with a weird aftertaste. "Water." I gasp out. Brady walks the short distance to the fridge and grabs me a bottle of spring water. He twists off the cap before handing it to me.

In my haste to take a sip I spill some down my chin and onto the tops of my breasts. Brady's eyes track the beads of moisture and I squeeze my thighs together. I want his tongue and lips there sucking them up.

I gulp the water down so fast I choke on it. More water spills from between my lips as I sputter, trying to hold in my cough. Somehow, I swallow the remainder in my mouth before I erupt into a hacking fit of coughing. Tears pour from my eyes and it takes me a full minute to stop.

"Are you okay?" Brady asks, a look of concern on his handsome face. I nod my head and hold up a finger. I can feel how red my face has become and I'm sure my already smudged makeup is now messily trailing down my cheeks. I wipe under each eye as I catch my breath.

Fuck my life. I won't have to remind myself to forget about Brady because he's never going to want to see me again. Right about now it must be registering with him what a disaster I am.

The coughing fit settles down until it's a sporadic single cough here and there.

"You sure you're okay?" he asks his eyebrow raised.

"Yeah, I'm fine. It just went down the wrong pipe." I don't know why I feel the need to explain. Hasn't everyone choked on a drink at some point?

"I'm going to call a cab now. Thanks for taking care of me last night." I take a step back and move to turn around when his large fingers close around my upper arm stopping me in my tracks.

"You don't need a cab, I'll take you home. What's the rush, kitten?" I glance at his hand wrapped around my arm. Those same hands work magic on the football field. I bet they work magic in the bedroom too.

Don't go there, Harlow.

"I have a project I need to work on." My eyes shift, looking around the kitchen, afraid he'll see the lie reflected in them. Thankfully, he doesn't push.

"Let me grab some sneakers and my keys and we'll hit the road. I don't want to interfere with your perfect GPA." He grins crookedly, a quick glimpse of his dimple appears, before he walks away.

My hand goes to my chest and I close my eyes as I take a few long, slow breaths. How am I supposed to resist him when he's flashing his dimple in my face? I'm going to stop looking at him altogether.

"Here." He walks back into the kitchen. Our fingers touch as he passes me my phone, my fake I.D and the twenty dollar bill I brought to the bar. "This was in the pocket of your jeans when I washed them." I don't think I've ever been so aware of a guy before. Every contact or interaction we have seems magnified.

Maybe I'm just turning the strong attraction I feel for him into something more.

"Thanks. I'd be screwed if I lost this." I hold up my phone. "My stepmom would have my head and guilt trip me for the rest of my life if she had to buy me a new one." I push it all down into my front pocket.

Following him out to his vehicle, I'm surprised when the lights flash on a nearby white Chevy Tahoe as he unlocks it with his keyless entry. He opens the door for me and puts his hand on my arm to assist me up. Once I'm settled, he closes me in and gets in the driver's side.

I rattle off my address and we're on our way. My apartment is located only five minutes from his. If I wasn't still feeling under the weather from being hungover I could've walked home. As it was, I was so drunk on the taxi ride to his place I didn't realize how close he lives to me.

When he parks curbside in front of my building I jump out before he's even shifted into park.

"What – no hug?" he jokes.

"Thanks for the ride home, Brady." My hand is on the door, ready to close it.

"Say that again," he tells me with a smile.

"What?" I question confused at what he wants.

"My name." He smirks. "I like hearing you say it."

I roll my eyes and slam the door shut. Quickly spinning around, I head for the front door. I don't want him to know how much it excites me when he says those kinds of things. I don't think I can stop this attraction I feel for him. I'm going to avoid him at all costs. It's the easiest solution.

CHAPTER FIVE

BRADY

Football practice has been kicking my ass every single day this week. There's an important divisional game this coming weekend. Coach has been working us over time in preparation for what's sure to be a battle. I've been too tired to do anything but eat, sleep and go to class. Even making it there's been a struggle.

I haven't seen Harlow at all. She's like a ghost on campus. I never seem to notice her, but I don't understand how it's possible. She's so fucking gorgeous she's impossible to miss. *Why am I not seeing her?*

I made sure I grabbed her number when I had her phone the other night. I wasn't taking any chances on losing touch with her. I've tried texting her, but she ignores the messages I send. Glancing down at my cellphone, I read through the most recent ones I sent.

Me – *Hey.* Nothing. I tried again.

Me – *Hey, it's that gorgeous guy you secretly like.* Still nothing. I sent another.

Me – You *and me eating dinner together. Great idea, right?* Still nothing. She's ignored them. I'm not used to being ignored. I tried again, just in case.

Me – *You're giving me a complex here.*

It doesn't help my situation any that I have her number and she's not answering. I'm going to wait until this weekend and if I haven't bumped into her by then or successfully reached her on the phone, then I'm going to swing by her place. She can't avoid me forever. There's no way in hell I'll let this girl slip away.

Game day rolls around and I'm feeling great. Coach has us well prepared for this team. We've watched a lot of videos of our opponent and we know their offense and defense inside out. That's a great feeling going into a game – to know all you need to do is play the best you can and your team should come out on top.

My warm up goes well. My arm is feeling solid today. When I head into the locker room it's alive with the sound of laughter as my teammates rib and joke with each other. I slowly chew on a protein bar and drink some water, getting lost in thoughts of Harlow as I relax down onto the locker room bench. I wonder what she's doing tonight. Is she home studying for midterms or is she out with some other guy? This thought just about guts me. I don't want anyone else to touch her – only me. I pinch the bridge of my nose and drop my chin to my chest. I picture Harlow standing in front of me in tight jeans with one of my jerseys knotted at her waist. Fuck. I'd like to see her wearing my number eight and nothing else.

"Okay boys," coach walks in the locker room clapping his hands to get our attention. "It's time to put all the hard work we've logged in this week, to use," he begins his pregame pep talk and I focus on what he's saying. By the time he's done we all feel invincible and as if this win is ours if we want it bad enough.

"Everything okay man?" Nick asks, sliding onto the bench beside me.

"Yeah, why do you ask?"

"You seem a little off - a little distracted. Just making sure your head's in good place."

I hold my fist out for him to bump. "Yeah, it's all good, bro."

Harlow. I conjure up her image one more time before pushing her to the back of my mind.

I've got a game to win.

We end the first half up by seven, a much smaller cushion than we were hoping for. Their D-line has been kicking my ass up and down the field. I'm sore and fucking pissed off. I'm not one to point fingers, but my O-line has been crumbling and missing their blocks which is why I'm getting pummeled in the first place. We're playing like shit - like an unprepared high school team nervously scrambling around. Our only saving grace is our defense has been doing a great job of shutting their offense down.

Stretching my legs out straight in front of me, I grimace. Fuck. My right knee is killing me. It's an old skateboarding injury from my teen years and every once in a while it flares up. I don't have time for this bullshit. There's still half the game left and there's no way in hell I'm not playing in it. I take a sip of water and lean my head back raising my face to the sky. I breathe deep and tell myself to focus. I'm usually pretty good at remaining positive in the face of adversity, but today I'm struggling. *We're winning, why am I being such a negative asshole?*

Harlow's face flashes into my thoughts. This girl has me tied in knots and I need to do something about it. The way I see it there are two options for me. One, I can bang her and get it out of my system or two, I can just forget about her and bang someone else. The second is probably the smarter way to go. It's not like she's ever going to give me the time of day anyhow. Guzzling down the rest of the water, I chuck the bottle to the trash barrel next to the bench. I scrub my hands up and down my face.

Harlow Summers is just a pipe dream which will never come to fruition. Football's what matters to me. *I need to get my head back in this game.*

Pacing back and forth along the sidelines, trying to keep my knee limber my eyes move to the scoreboard. It's fourteen all and we're only going to have time for one more possession. Defense has done their job and held it to a tied game.

Rolling my shoulders a few times, I tip my head side to side, loosening my neck muscles. The adrenaline's starting to kick in. I can feel it coursing through my body. There's a sense of urgency in the air. We need to score.

Glancing at the fans in the stands who came to support us today, I recognize some who never miss a game. I'm grateful to play for such a great university.

I let my eyes rove over all the nameless people in the section of the stands behind our bench. One person stands out amongst them all. Harlow Summers. *She's here.*

My heart pounds as I study her. She's dressed in a black wool coat with a red scarf wrapped around her neck and matching gloves. I smile when I realize she has on white earmuffs. She's so fucking cute. Her thick, dark brown hair is the biggest thing on her small frame. I rake my teeth over my bottom lip and wonder why she's here? Cracking my knuckles, I watch her until she senses my stare. When her large gray eyes find me she doesn't react. She sits frozen in place. I flash a large grin and point a finger in her direction, making it impossible for her to deny being here.

It's show time. Time to win this game and crush our opponent's hope.

Pulling my helmet back on, I fasten the chin strap as I stalk back on the field, determination in every step I take. Ten plays later Nick catches a perfect pass in the end zone for the game winning touchdown. We ran down the clock so well, with seconds left all that's left to do is take a knee.

We finish the final play, the cheers of the large crowd resonating in my ears. I hug my teammates and enjoy a few moments of celebration, but then my eyes immediately go to where Harlow was seated. She's no longer there. Scanning the area for a flash of her bright red scarf, I find her halfway up the stairs, her back to me, in the throng of people. Disappointment washes over me. I was hoping to talk with her for a few minutes and thank her for coming to watch. Maybe even use my mad powers of persuasion to convince her to go out with me later.

She did come to the game - to an away game, after admitting she doesn't like or follow football. The only reason I can think of for her being here today is to see me. My chest swells. She wants me bad, but she's still a bit innocent. I need to pull the words right out of her, like an exorcist. I'll do whatever she needs me to. Christ, I'll dip my wick in holy water if I need to.

The bus ride back home is never louder than when we win a divisional game. Typically, I'd be all up in the commotion, but right now my head is back on the headrest and my eyes are shut while thoughts of Harlow play on a nonstop reel in my mind. What's my next step going to be? I should figure out a game plan. I need to be methodical.

The voices around me bleed through my concentration.

"I'm taking her out tonight. She's a live one," Cameron boasts in the arrogant tone of voice he pulls off so well. My ears perk up. Is he talking about Raine?

"She was a wildcat the other night. I think my back still has the scratches to show for it." Opening my eyes to slits, I see him flash a grin at Jason, one of the offensive lineman, before typing on his cellphone.

"I'm trying to get her to bring her hot little roommate. I wouldn't mind tapping her ass too." The answering beep of a text has his head dropping down to peer at the screen. It keeps him from seeing the expression of rage on my face. He's not going to be within five fucking feet of Harlow. Not if I've anything to say about it. I want to creep across the aisle, grip him by the nape of his neck and slam his face into the seat in front of him. I want to, but I don't. I can't. It would mean being benched for a game or two which would hurt our team exponentially. Our back up QB is good, but he's not me. I know I can be a screw up sometimes, but football is the one thing I don't fuck around with. It's my life.

Sitting up in my seat I lean in Cameron's direction. "Where are you guys going tonight? I could stand to blow off some steam." I rake my teeth over my bottom lip.

"We're going to C's Pub. You should come." He flicks a glance in my direction before typing on his phone some more. He has no idea how close I was to kicking his ass only seconds ago.

I lean my head back, smiling to myself. *I'll be seeing you real soon, Harlow.*

CHAPTER SIX

BRADY

The November night air is cold as we walk down the sidewalk along Commonwealth Ave. My hands are jammed in the front pockets of my jeans and I can see my breath with every exhale. My roommates Zeke and Nick are with me, neither of them had other plans.

After about five minutes of shivering in only a hooded sweatshirt, I see the iconic red letters on the front of the building - C's Pub. The three of us have been coming here since we were freshman. Considered to be a Boston University pub, it's conveniently located with access to the T. We don't need to take the train. Our apartment is close enough for us to walk here, and stumble home which is the main reason why we're frequent patrons.

The interior is dimly lit and loaded with people, many of them students and twenty-somethings who work in the area. My eyes trek around the room, looking for Cameron and the rest of our teammates. They're all sizeable guys and should be pretty easy to pick out in the crowd.

Spotting them gathered around the other end of the bar, we head in their direction. As usual, the three of us are bombarded with people wanting to say hi, or girls who are hoping to be the ones to go home with us. I nod and smile, keeping it brief. There's a reason for being here tonight and she's very much in the forefront of my mind.

Exchanging a barrage of fist bumps and high fives with our teammates we flag the waitress down and order some beers. Scanning the immediate group with my eyes, I'm disappointed when there's no sign of Harlow. Fuck. I was really hoping I'd get a chance to see her tonight. How am I supposed to get to know this girl if I never talk to her?

Once there's a beer in my hand I decide to make the most of the night and enjoy myself with the guys. We had a big win today; it's time to celebrate.

"Did you see my skills on the final catch?" Nick asks, flexing his arms.

I laugh and take a sip of my beer before answering. "Bullshit. That pass was a well-aimed rocket that dropped right into your hands."

"I've got to agree with Linc on this one. That pass couldn't have been more perfect," Zeke offers clinking the neck of his bottle against mine.

Raising the beer to my lips once more my eyes move down the length of the long bar until they freeze on the most beautiful girl I've ever seen. *She came.* Using this opportunity to study her while she's not aware, my eyes take in the long, dark, curly hair draping sexily around her like a blanket. I want to be wrapped up in that hair with her; cocooned from the world and completely lost in each other. Picturing the two of us in my bed, her hair spilling all around me as she leans down to join our mouths has my dick twitching.

I need to know what her lips feel like, what she tastes like.

"Earth to Linc," Zeke jokes, laughing. He follows the path of my gaze and then elbows me in the side. "Close your mouth bro, you're drooling."

My eyes briefly flick to him before returning to Harlow. "So it's like that is it?" Zeke states, smirking at me.

I raise an eyebrow at him, downing the rest of my beer. Holding the empty up I point to it, signaling to the waitress I need another.

I slam the bottle down on the bar and turn to Zeke. "Like what?" I ask, playing dumb. I'm not ready to hear any shit about Harlow. I'm not sure what this overpowering attraction I feel for her is and I'm definitely not ready to talk about it with anyone.

"You like her." He tips his chin in Harlow's direction. "I think it's cute man. The infamous Brady Lincoln finally has his dick in a twist over a girl." He grips my shoulder in his meaty hand. "Didn't I just say you'd meet someone who would knock you on your ass? I'm like a fucking prophet," Zeke jokes. "From now on you need to refer to me as Prophet Zeke. I'll have more wisdom to impart after I drink about ten more of these." He points at his beer. I shake my head and laugh.

"Fuck that. You're still the same donkey who fell for Amber Marcell freshman year," I retort, reminding him about an ex who cheated on him. We all told him she was trash, but he 'loved her,' and was convinced she felt the same. It wasn't until he caught her fucking Cameron in her dorm room that he finally believed what we'd been telling him all along.

"Low blow Linc. Thanks for bringing up all the painful memories." He pretends to wipe a tear from his eye and I laugh.

"Yeah, you loved her so much it only took you until later that night to get over her. You were balls deep in some blonde within hours of breaking up with her." The waitress hands me my beer. The bottle is icy cold in my hand. "I should know, I walked in on the two of you going at it in our dorm room." Taking a sip from my bottle I shake my head. "I got an up close and personal look at your hairy ass. I think I'm still scarred from it." Shuddering at the memory I let my eyes search out Harlow. She's no longer near the door. I find her in the middle of my teammates standing next to Cameron and her friend, Raine.

My feet are in motion before I even realize it. Cameron leans down to speak to her, his lips near her ear and my blood boils. He needs to back the fuck off. He won't be able to run any touchdowns in with a busted knee.

Harlow leans away from him, looking uncomfortable. I react without even thinking. Stopping in front of her, I take her hand in mine. Her eyes get wide when she sees me and the merest hint of a smile teases the corners of her mouth.

I wink at her. "Sorry to interrupt, but I need to borrow Harlow for a little while." I don't even look at Cameron. Turning to walk off, I tug her along with me. Moving through the crowd, her hand in mine, I seek out a place where we can talk.

At the back of the bar is a wide hallway leading to the restrooms and the rear exit. I pull her in there and then press her back into the wall. "Are you here with Cameron?" I question, my voice coming out harsher than I intend. The thought of her anywhere near that asshole has me tied up in knots.

"No, I'm here with Raine. I didn't even want to come." Staring up at me with her big gray eyes, she chews on her bottom lip.

I expel a big sigh, closing my eyes for a moment. When I open them she's staring at my mouth. Fuck. *Don't look at me like that, kitten. That look can get you in a lot of trouble.* Her tongue peeks out and traces along her plump bottom lip. I feel my resistance crumbling and there's nothing I can do about it.

My hands slide into her hair, tangling themselves up in her long silk like tresses. I hold her head in place and stare into her stormy gray eyes. Slowly moving closer, I lower my lips toward hers. Kissing her is inevitable. This was meant to happen. I connect our mouths and her soft lips part as her tongue snakes out to tentatively touch mine. Her kiss isn't the kiss of someone with a lot of experience. My dick gets agonizingly hard, thinking about how much fun it will be to corrupt her in the most satisfying way.

One of my hands slides down her spine, caressing over the curve of her hip and down to cup her ass in my large palm. Oh Fuck. Her ass is heart shaped perfection. I can't wait to grip it while she's riding my cock and slap it while she's bent over on all fours. Head down, ass in the air will look good on her.

Bending my knees, I scoop her up, dick in line with her pussy. Grinding into her, I use the wall for leverage. She moans into my mouth and digs her fingernails into the top of my shoulders as our tongues rub against each other. I can't get enough of her. I want more, but this is not the place to take it.

I tear my mouth from hers, fighting for the next breath. "Come home with me," I say, a pleading tone in my voice.

"I can't." Her eyes move around the hallway. "I'm here with Raine." Her cheeks are flushed an attractive pink shade. I like knowing I'm not the only one affected by our kiss.

"I think we both know Raine's going to be busy with Cameron." I stare down into her stormy gray eyes.

"I know, but it doesn't change that I'm here with her. If she leaves with him, I'll go home," she informs me.

I frame her face with my hands. "I want to spend some time together and learn more about you. Nothing else has to happen." My eyes implore her to see I mean what I'm saying. I don't know why it's so important for me to be with her; I just know it is. "Please come home with me."

I've never had to beg a girl to leave with me before. Usually, I don't need to ask twice, but with every interaction we engage in I realize how different Harlow is from all the other girls I've met.

"Okay," she whispers so softly I think I'm hearing things.

I raise an eyebrow. "Yes?" I question.

"Yes," she answers a small smile on her pink lips. Flashing her a grin, I grab her hand. I'm getting her the hell out of here before she changes her mind.

Walking in the cold night air, probably wasn't on her agenda, but having her cuddled up to my side, my arm wrapped around her shoulders, feels fucking awesome. This might be the first time I wish we didn't live so close to C's. I want to stay like this for as long as possible. She's not fighting our closeness, she seems to be relishing it. I'm sure it's out of necessity, but whatever the motivation is, she's still here, where I want her to be.

"You're a sophomore, right?" I question. At her nod, I continue. "Where are you from?"

"I grew up in Rhode Island. My stepmother still lives there."

"Are you glad you chose BU? Was it your top school?"

She nods her head. "Yep, I always dreamed of coming here. My parents brought me to Boston for a long weekend as a kid. I fell in love with the city and from then on I dreamed of attending college here. Some of my favorite memories are from that weekend."

The questions I'm asking are mundane, but I don't know how to do this. How do you get to know a girl beyond sex?

I run my hand through my hair. I've never done this before and never cared enough to put the effort in. I glance down at her upturned face; I hope it gets easier with time.

Directing her up the front steps of the brick and mortar brownstone where I live, I unlock the main door and usher her inside out of the cold.

She rubs her palms together searching for any warmth she can find. I take her hand and lead her through the open space of the main entryway and over to our first-floor apartment. Key in hand, I unlock and open the door as quickly as possible.

She enters first; I follow behind, eyes swinging down to her ass. I remind myself I need to behave. No matter how difficult it is - no matter how much I want to lick every inch of her tempting body, I need to act like a fucking boy scout.

"What do you want to drink?" I ask kicking off my shoes by the door. "We have beer, and just about every liquor you could want."

She presses her lips together as she thinks about what she wants. "I'll take a water, please."

"Give me your jacket and you can go get comfortable." Helping her to remove it, I hear the song 'Let's Get It On,' playing in my head. *Stop it, boy scout -remember?* I hang it on an empty hook next to the door and lift my chin in the direction of our large black leather couch in the living room. "Have a seat and I'll be right there."

Slowly she walks across the floor, the soles of her red converse quiet against the hardwood. I shake my head disgusted with myself and move into the kitchen to grab our drinks. Standing with the refrigerator door open, I allow the cool air to wash over me. Being in her company without trying to get her clothes off is going to be a challenge. Especially, when seeing her naked is on the top of my list of goals. I grab a beer and a bottle of water, then use my forearm to close the fridge.

Harlow is lost on our large couch. The top of her head barely peeks over the back edge. She's kicked her shoes off and her feet are up on the coffee table. I smile as I come around the front and notice her socks are light pink and have the Patriots logo on them.

"Here you go." Handing her the bottle, I sit down next to her. She shrinks into herself when my thigh touches hers. Her water clutched in her hands, her elbows tucked into her sides, reflects how uncomfortable my presence makes her. *Fuck.*

"Let's watch some TV." Grabbing the remote, I flip through the channels. *What kind of shows does she like?* She probably likes some wholesome, do gooder shit I'll have to suffer through.

"Wait. Go back." Her voice interrupts my thoughts. I flip back a channel, then another, not really paying any mind.

"Yes," she says excitement in her tone. My eyes flick to her, taking in the big smile on her face. I glance at the screen to see what has her so enthusiastic. *No fucking way.* Patriots All Access, one of my favorite shows is on.

I take a gulp of my beer, my heart pounds out of control in my chest. This girl is fucking perfect and the more I find out about her the more I want to know. This is some scary shit for a guy who's never held a meaningful conversation with a woman before.

"You like Patriots All Access? I thought you hated football?" I question, my eyebrow raised.

"I used to watch every episode with my dad." She smiles, a sheepish expression on her face. "I may have lied about not liking football. I love the Pats." She sips on her water, her eyes glued to the TV as highlights of the past week's game are being discussed and plays are being diagramed.

"Yeah I figured. Your socks kind of gave you away." I nudge her foot with mine. "Do you guys still watch it together when you're home?" I ask, resting my beer on my thigh.

Her eyebrows draw together in a small frown. "No, my dad passed away when I was sixteen."

Fuck. I wish I could go back thirty seconds and ask her another question.

"I'm sorry. I didn't mean to bring up tough memories," I quickly apologize.

She shakes her head, then glances at me. "It's okay. I miss him, but I'm fine with talking about it."

"What happened to him?" I ask. I want to learn as much as I can about her. I don't know if I'll get another opportunity like this. Tonight, might be my one chance to get to know her before she hides from me again.

"He died in a car accident."

"That had to be tough for you. You were young, only in high school." I take a sip of beer, hoping the alcohol will help make me a better conversationalist. So far, it's not helping.

"It was, but it does get easier to think about him the more time passes."

"Who's your favorite Patriots player?" I ask, changing the subject.

"Edelman," she replies.

"Because you think he's hot, right?" I question, shaking my head. Nothing ruins football for me more than having a woman watch the game with me. Been there done that. I don't want to hear about the player's asses or how hot the team is.

I made a no females rule in our apartment for game days. Watching my team in peace is a top priority. My boys need all my focus to win. They're counting on me.

She laughs. "No, he's my favorite because he's awesome. He's had ninety-eight receptions so far this season, but the best thing about him is his bromance with Tom Brady."

I stare at her in complete awe. *Who the fuck is this girl?* She's like a beautiful alien. I've heard they exist, but never had any proof they do. One thing is certain; she's one of a kind.

.

CHAPTER SEVEN

HARLOW

I burrow my cheek further into the warm cushion I'm lying on. Inhaling, I smell the pine scent of men's cologne and my eyes snap open. Holding still, I move my eyeballs only. Glancing down at the surface I've been napping on, I realize it's Brady's chest. Oh crap. My eyes scroll up his muscular pecs to his thick neck and finally to his face. I breathe a sigh of relief when I realize he's asleep.

I move slowly, gently easing his hand from where it rests on my hip, lowering it down to the cushion. Carefully raising my torso, I scoot to the edge of the couch. Sliding on my Converse before rising to my feet, I head toward the door. I'm grabbing my jacket from the wall hook when I hear Brady stirring.

"Harlow," he softly says my name. *Shit.* Hurriedly shoving my arms in the sleeves of my coat, I don't answer.

His head swivels to the side. Catching me in his periphery he twists his torso around. "Where are you going?" His voice is hoarse from his nap and impossibly sexy. He rubs the sleep from his eyes with his fists like a little boy, and my stomach flutters. He's so much different than I expected him to be.

"I'm going home," I say, pulling on some blue gloves I had stashed away in one of my jacket pockets.

He smoothly rises to his feet. "I'll walk you home. You shouldn't be out at night by yourself in the city."

I look him over as he walks in my direction. His dark blonde hair is a mess and his sweatshirt is wrinkled from where I was lying on it. He's never looked more tempting to me. *Why does he have to be so attractive?* When our eyes meet mine awkwardly bounce away.

Reaching past me, he grabs a black winter vest from a hook and shrugs it on. He pulls on a black knit cap and shoves his keys in one of the front pockets on his jeans before sliding on some sneakers.

Opening the door, he gestures. "After you."

"Thank you," I murmur as I walk past and start toward the exit. The sound of the door closing behind me startles me. Being in his company has me on edge. *I just need to make it through the next five minutes and then I'll be safe inside my dorm.*

I make it outside and down the front steps before he catches up with me. He slings an arm around my shoulder like it's the most natural thing in the world. Maybe for him it's not a big deal, but for me it is. I can barely breathe from his nearness. The scent of his cologne wraps around us and the heat of his arm is both comforting and nerve wracking. I know he's a lot more affectionate with the opposite sex than I am. I won't allow myself to make a big deal out of this even though my stomach is fluttering with excitement. It's perfectly normal for him to sleep with random people so why would an arm around my shoulders mean anything?

We remain silent the entire walk, until I pull my keys out of my pocket.

"When can I see you again?" he asks, a crooked smile on his lips.

Now. My body shouts silently. "I don't think that's a good idea." I play with the ring of keys, the sound of the metal jingling. I stare at them as if they're the most fascinating thing I've ever seen.

He steps forward, crowding me until my nose is practically buried against his chest. Plucking the keys from me with one hand, he tips my chin up with the other. His blue eyes stare into my gray ones. I exhale with a wavering sigh. I know he's not going to make this easy on me.

"I want to take you out and you want me to. Whether you'll admit it or not is another story." He smirks.

He's such a cocky bastard. I want to refuse him and give his ego some much needed bruises.

I want to.

I should.

But I can't.

I really like him; even though I see hazard lights flashing in my mind every time I think of giving him a chance.

"Come on. Haven't I been a perfect gentleman so far?" His expression is exaggeratedly innocent. I shake my head.

"You're killing me here. Do I need to get down on my knees and beg you?" He starts to lower down to the sidewalk in front of my dorm.

"No," I shout, gripping his arm. "You don't need to." The last thing I need is someone seeing Brady on his knees in front of me.

"I've never dated anyone before." He shakes his head. "I really like you and I'm hoping you'll give me a chance to take you out."

I chew on my bottom lip, nodding my head slightly.

"Does this mean you'll go out with me tomorrow night?" He pulls his sleeve up and glances at his watch. "Actually, it is tomorrow now," he comments taking note of the time. "Can I take you out tonight?"

I lick my lips and then press them together drawing out the moment. I'm not strong enough to refuse him, but I can make him sweat it out a little.

He tips his head and raises an eyebrow as if to say - what's it going to be?

I don't answer. I hold out my hand. "Keys, please."

An expression of doubt briefly flickers in his eyes before he gently places them in my palm.

Spinning around I start down the walkway leading to the front door.

"Hey," he yells.

I stop and turn to face him. "I'm just messing with you. We can go out tonight."

He stalks toward me. *Oh god.* He grips both my arms and tugs me into his chest. My breath leaves me as every inch of our bodies is plastered together from groin to the tips of my breasts. One of his hands slides to the middle of my back and continues down until it caresses over the curve of my hip.

"Not so funny now is it, naughty girl," he growls. Cupping one of my ass cheeks in his big hand, he squeezes it. His mouth swoops down to take mine in a hot, wet kiss that has me thinking of being naked with him as soon as possible. His tongue thrusts against mine. Gripping the back of his neck, I wish I didn't have gloves on. I want to feel his warm skin under my fingertips.

He pulls away, his breathing labored. "You need to get inside before I throw you over my shoulder and take you back to my place."

My cheeks flush red at the vision his words conjure up. Stepping back, I nod. "I'll see you tonight."

"Eight o'clock. I'll be right here, waiting," he says, pointing at the spot he's standing in.

"Okay." I pivot and practically float to the door.

I have a date with Brady Lincoln, I have a date with Brady Lincoln, I have a date with Brady Lincoln.

I peek over my shoulder at him as I'm about to go inside. "See ya." I awkwardly wave.

He doesn't answer me. Instead, flashing his damn irresistible smirk at me. *I'm so screwed.*

Watching the clock tick down until it's eight o'clock, has kept me occupied for the past thirty minutes. I don't want to appear too eager, but I am. Going out with him is all I've thought about since he walked me home last night. I've replayed our kiss about a thousand times and each time it seemed even hotter.

Will he kiss me again tonight? I hope so.

I inhale a deep breath to compose myself as I push open the door to my building. There's a moment where the nervous flutters in my stomach take over.

Will he be there waiting?

What if he changed his mind and he doesn't show?

Relief washes over me. All the worry is for nothing. He's standing in the exact spot he said he'd be. His hands are in his jeans pockets, broad shoulders rolled forward in the gray B.U. hoodie he wears so well. We had an unseasonably warm day for November and it's carried over into tonight.

Happiness overtakes me and bursts out of me with a huge smile. I couldn't contain if I tried.

He moves forward and I do the same, meeting him halfway.

"Hi." He smiles and pulls me in for a hug.

"Hi," I say, my greeting muffled against his sweatshirt. He kisses me on the top of my head. It reminds me of my dad. He's the only who's ever done this. I blink back the sting of tears. Now's not the time to turn into an emotional mess. I'm sure for him it was just a reflex and not some declaration of his feelings for me. I pride myself on being practical and logical. I refuse to turn into one of those girls who thinks if a guy says hello to her or holds the door it means a lifetime commitment.

Pulling away, he holds me at arm's length. Sweeping his eyes over me, he slowly studies me from the tip of my head down to my converse covered feet. I flush from his stare.

"You look beautiful," he tells me. I appreciate the compliment, but I know I'm not dressed to impress tonight. I'm wearing my most comfortable jeans and my favorite black sweater.

"Thanks, you look pretty good yourself, but you don't need me to tell you."

"I like hearing you compliment me. I think this might be the first time you have."

Rolling my eyes, I reply, "I don't need to feed your ego, it's hefty enough already. In fact, that sucker could use a diet."

He chuckles. "I've a feeling you'll be the one to lighten the load so to speak." He holds his hand out for me. "Come on. Let's get some dinner. I'm starving."

Placing my hand in his, I walk beside him. The soles on my shoes scuffing over the jagged cracks in the concrete as we head down the sidewalk.

"How do you feel about pizza? Do you love it or just like it?"

My nose scrunches at his words. "Doesn't everyone love pizza?" I question, glancing up at him - glancing way up at him. He's so tall. He has to be at least six foot three.

"Actually, Zeke doesn't like pizza. I almost considered finding a new roommate freshman year because of that anomaly. But, then I realized he was the perfect person to room with because it meant I didn't have to share my pizza. And I can eat a lot."

I giggle and he flashes me a quick grin. He taps his head with his index finger. "Sometimes you need to look at the bigger picture." He glances down at me. "Take us for instance," he pauses. "I know going out with me didn't seem like such a great idea at first, but now you must see the value."

My eyes flick up to him, one eyebrow raised skeptically. "I do?" I question.

"Sure, you do. You already know I'll keep you warm when I walk you home. I'll never push you to do something you don't want to. I love pizza and so do you. I can get you tickets to any football game you want." I open my mouth to reply and he shakes his head. "Don't even go there. I saw you at the game *miss I don't like football or football players.*" He smirks and then his expression changes. It becomes serious and heated, his blue eyes burning into mine. "Our chemistry is off the charts. The kisses we've shared have been fucking phenomenal. I'm getting hard just thinking about them."

"Brady," I shout, my cheeks hot with an embarrassed flush.

"What?" he questions. "I'm just stating the facts. I prefer to be direct." He stops walking and tugs my hand. I crash into him and a high-pitched squeak leaves me.

Cupping my face, his palms are warm against my cheeks. He stares intently in my eyes. "I plan to have you, any way I can. If that means taking you out for three months straight before I get to kiss you again, then that's exactly what I'll do. But I'm hoping you won't make me wait too long."

Our eyes remain locked in a tension filled stare off. I couldn't look away, if I tried.

I want to kiss him. *Should I?* Chewing on my lip, I'm lost in indecision. I'm not sure what to do or say. I've never been in a situation like this before. And before I can decide he interrupts.

"You ready for that pizza now?"

CHAPTER EIGHT

BRADY

"Have you ever eaten here before?"

She shakes her head, her gray eyes open wide as she takes in the lively atmosphere of Gino's.

"It takes a little while to get used to the noise level and all the people. Their pizza is worth the assault on your ears, I promise." I smile as my eyes sweep around the room. This is one of my favorite places to come for dinner. I end up here at least twice a week, sometimes more.

"Wow, it must be pretty amazing pizza if it's worth suffering hearing loss." She smiles.

"I don't want to influence your opinion. I'll let you be the judge."

The waitress stops beside our table. Steam rises from the thick layer of mozzarella cheese as she sets the pan down in the middle of the table.

"Can I get you anything else?" she asks.

Harlow smiles and shakes her head.

"We're all set, thanks." She walks away and my gaze settles back on the gorgeous girl across from me. "Dig in. I can't wait to see what you think." My eyebrows raise as I wait for her to take the first bite.

"I feel like there should be a drum roll or something," she jokes. Picking up the oversized slice with both of her hands, she raises it to her lips. I watch in envy as she blows on it before the pointed end enters her mouth. I wish she was wrapping her lips around a certain appendage of mine.

Her eyes shut as she bites into the slice. When she begins to chew, a moan escapes her lips. I can't stop watching. The pizza is all but forgotten as I study her. I want my hands on her to be the reason she moans. I want to be the one who's repeatedly drawing them out of her.

Her eyes open and she flushes when she notices me taking her in.

"Would you like me to order my own pizza?" I joke.

She giggles, then places the piece down on her plate. Wiping her lips with the white cloth napkin she then answers me. "This is the best I've ever had. How is it possible I've never heard about this place?"

"A lot of the football team comes here. Which is how I learned of it freshman year." I bite off a large chunk of crust.

"At least I still have the rest of sophomore year to enjoy it and then two more. I think I'll be eating here a lot."

"I'm excited to be a senior next year. Only one more year of having this place easily accessible will suck." I take a sip of water, studying her over my glass. "I meant to ask you last night, what your major is?"

She finishes chewing, then answers. "I'm getting a psychology degree. I'm not sure what I want to do, but I know I'd like to help people through emotionally hard times." She takes a sip of her coke and wipes her mouth on her napkin. "What about you?"

"I'm going for communications." I shove the rest of the crust in my mouth and chew.

She nods. "You want to follow in your father's footsteps?"

I swallow past the lump in my throat her mentioning my dad brings up. "I want to play football in the NFL and then get into broadcasting like him, but that's where the similarities will end." I wipe my mouth with the napkin and throw it down on the table. "I don't want to be anything like him in any other way."

"I didn't mean to bring up a sore subject for you," she says, her expression apologetic.

"No, it's okay. I don't want to get into the dysfunction of my family yet. Let's save that for another time." I wink hoping to lighten the mood.

Shit. I didn't mean to reveal anything about my father. I don't like to talk about what he's done to our family. When he and my mom were married, he couldn't keep his dick in his pants. She would forgive him every time. It wasn't until I was three years old that they split for good and only because his mistress was pregnant with my little brother, Trevor.

My dad's been a better father figure to him than he ever was to me. He and I don't always see eye to eye. He has his plan for my future and it doesn't follow the same path mine does.

"So, where are you taking me after this?"

"Who said we're going anywhere else? Pizza's not a good enough date for you?"

"I..," she sputters at a loss for words.

I chuckle. "I'm just kidding. I'm taking you to a party. I want to introduce you to some of my friends."

She presses her lips together. "What's wrong?" I ask before grabbing another slice from the tray.

She scrunches her nose up. "I'm not sure that's a good idea."

My eyebrow raises and I pause with the slice of pizza halfway to my mouth. "Going to a party?" She nods her head.

"Why not?" I question.

"Because you're you." She gestures to me with her hand.

My eyebrows draw together. "What does that mean?" Placing my slice down on the plate, I continue. "Why does who I am matter?"

"You're the quarterback of the football team. Everyone knows who you are and I'm not comfortable being on display."

"You didn't know who I was. Who's to say you're the only one?"

A sheepish look passes over her face.

"Wait a minute." I lean my arms on the table. "Did you know who I was that night at the party?"

Her eyes lower to her plate and when they move up to meet mine they're filled with humor. "I might've known who you were." She shrugs her shoulders.

I rake my teeth over my bottom lip. "I think there's a lot more to you than anyone knows." I study her and slowly nod my head. "Much more than you let everyone see. It's going to be a lot of fun discovering all those hidden layers." I flash her a grin.

Her hand squeezes mine when we enter the frat house the party is being held at. I'm almost positive it was only a reflex on her part, a burst of nervous energy. I tighten my hold and hope it helps to calm her. It's obvious she's uncomfortable. Her eyes are cast downward and she's pulled my arm in front of her like a shield to protect her from all the people she doesn't know.

I lean down, my lips next to her ear. "Relax. You're with me," I reassure her.

She manages a small closed lipped smile in reply.

I know she's apprehensive about being here. Pulling her to the side of the room, I tuck her in front of me and lean back against the wall. My arms are loose around her narrow waist. Lowering down, I peer into her eyes. "Harlow, I want you to have a good time while we're here. You need to stop worrying about everyone else and focus on me." I flash her a quick grin. "You can stay as close to me as you want." I raise my eyebrows up and down and she giggles. "That's what I'm talking about. I want to see your beautiful smile." My hands move up to cup her shoulders. "We can leave any time you want. Just give me the signal."

"What's the signal?" she asks a curious expression on her face.

Rubbing my chin, I think of what it can be.

"Just tell me you want some alone time with me. Those words will get me out of here in flash."

She slaps my chest. "Brady," she says rolling her eyes.

"Okay, that might not be the best one, but just for the record, I'd love to hear those words come out of your sexy mouth."

She looks away as a flush of pink washes over her fair skin.

"I've got it," I say.

Her eyes return to me.

"What if you just tell me you're ready to go? Good communication is important in relationships. We should always be upfront and honest with each other." Internally I grimace at my words. I've no fucking idea about relationships and all I learned from my parents are lies and mistrust. "What do you think?" Can you do that?"

She nods her head. "I can."

My hand slides from her shoulder, my fingers skimming over the back of her arm to clasp her hand. "Come on. I want to introduce you to some friends."

We maneuver through the crowded room toward Zeke's broad back and dark head. As we come upon the group of my friends I pull Harlow into my side, slinging my arm around her shoulders.

"Linc buddy, it's about time you showed," Zeke says. He smiles down at Harlow. "Now I see what the holdup was." He holds his hand out. "I'm Zeke, one of Brady's roommates."

Harlow tentatively places her hand in his and he pumps it up and down a few times jerking her around.

He releases his hold. "I'm sorry about that. I get a little carried away sometimes and you're just a little thing."

"Zeke, this is Harlow," I interject.

"Hi, it's nice to meet you," she politely replies and then shakes her hand as if she's in pain.

Zeke's eyes open wide. "Oh shit, did I hurt you?"

She giggles. "Just messing with you."

I bark out a laugh. For someone who was worried about meeting my friends she's jumped right in.

"Zeke is like a bull in a china shop. We call him Hulk because he doesn't know his own strength. "Hulk smash," I joke.

Harlow covers her mouth to hide her smile.

"I get no respect. Who protects your ass on the field every week?" He points at himself. "That would be me."

"Are you planning on introducing me at any point?" Claire, Zeke's girlfriend asks, placing a hand on his arm. Staring up at him, she pouts her lips. Zeke smiles down at her, falling for her ridiculous need to be the center of attention. She can do no wrong in his eyes and he won't listen to reason where she's concerned.

"Of course, babe. I'd never forget you," he says with a wink, before turning back to Harlow. "This gorgeous angel is my girlfriend Claire."

Harlow smiles. "Hi, it's nice to meet you."

Claire looks her over. "Hi," she says her tone cool and definitely not angel like.

Harlow reflexively leans into me.

Wrapping my arm around her shoulder, I pull her to my side. "Be nice, Claire. Harlow's important to me." My tone is light, but the seriousness in my expression gets the point across.

Claire's eyes flare with surprise before she answers. "I'm always nice, Brady."

I don't answer. Leaning down, my lips near Harlow's ear I say, "let's go get something to drink."

She nods her head.

"We'll be back in a bit. We're going to grab some drinks and I want to introduce Harlow to some of the other guys."

Zeke holds his fist out and I bump it with mine. "Later," I say then usher Harlow along with me toward the kitchen. We're at my old frat house, the same one I met her at a couple weeks ago. There are so many people here I end up taking Harlow's hand, keeping her slightly behind me as I shoulder us through the crowd. Nodding my head hello to those I know, I don't stop moving forward. I need a beer and I want to get a drink in her hand before she decides she's had enough of this madhouse and wants to leave.

When we reach the kitchen there's a crowd gathered around the table where Cameron and a few of my teammates are playing a game of strip poker with some of the cheerleaders. Judging by the noise level and the lack of clothes they've all started drinking the hard stuff early.

Harlow's eyes show how surprised she is at what we walked in on. I forget this is all new to her. Hell, this is tame compared to some of the shit that goes on here. There are a few cheerleaders who like to be watched. They'll suck anyone's dick on the football team and they don't care who sees. The larger the audience the better and they'll act like it's a fucking honor. Those are the girls I avoid. I might not be the most selective about who I fuck, but I do have some standards.

"What do you want to drink?" I ask, gesturing to the long line of bottles spread out on the granite counter.

I watch her eyes move over all the different kinds of liquor before she glances up at me.

"Do you have any wine coolers? I don't want anything that strong." Her teeth bite into her bottom lip with worry. "I don't usually drink," she adds.

I squeeze her hand, reassuring her. "No problem. Let me see what I can find." Releasing my hold on her I open the fridge and move things around until I find a berry wine cooler. I grimace. This bottle's probably been in here for four years. Does alcohol ever expire?

I search some more, but this is the only thing I come up with. Closing the door, I hand her the bottle.

She smiles. "Thanks. I've had this kind before. It's pretty good."

"Don't thank me yet. I'm not sure how long it's been buried inside our fridge. It could be from my freshman year."

She giggles and searches the bottle for an expiration date. "I don't see a date so I guess that means it never expires." She twists open the top, breaking the paper seal. "Here goes nothing. Cheers," she toasts before taking a sip. Once she swallows it all down she nods her head, pressing her lips together. "Tastes okay to me."

"You're taken care of. Now what am I in the mood for?" I spot a bottle of Captain Morgan spiced rum and add a good dose to some ice in a red cup. A little Coke goes in last and when I realize there's no straw in sight, I give it a stir with my index finger. I shrug my shoulders. "Desperate times call for desperate measures."

Harlow giggles as she watches me.

Pulling my finger from the cold beverage I hold it in front of her mouth. A complete look of panic comes over her face before she shakes her head.

Chuckling at her horrified expression, I dry my finger on her jeans. She jumps at my touch. "Calm down, kitten. I'm just joking. Believe me, my finger is not the body part I want you to suck."

She gasps, then covers her eyes with her hand.

I lean down, my lips close to her ear. "You do know I can still see you, right?" She shivers when she feels the heat of my breath fanning her skin with each word I say. I press a gentle kiss below her ear and run my nose along the graceful line of her neck. Her scent reminds me of a combination of strawberries and vanilla. "You smell delicious; good enough to eat. I can't wait to find out what you taste like," I growl.

She gasps again, lowering her hand down enough to reveal her large gray eyes. "Brady, you can't say things like that to me," she says, her voice so low it's barely audible.

Lifting my head, I peer in her eyes. "I just did." I wink, then continue in a more serious tone. "Harlow, I'm not saying anything I don't mean. I've been pretty clear on how I feel about you from the start." I take her hand from her face and place my cup down on the counter. Cradling her cheeks in my palms, I tell her, "I want you, plain and simple. I'm not going to pressure you into doing something you're not ready for, but I'm also going to be open about my feelings for you." I rub my nose against hers and then draw back. "I like you and I want to spend more time with you."

CHAPTER NINE

HARLOW

Did I hear him correctly? *He likes me?* My heart painfully thumps in my chest. I want to jump up and down like a pogo stick screaming with happiness. I can't believe Brady likes me. Now I don't know what to say to him. If I admit I like him back he'll wear me down and before you know it I'll be naked beneath him in bed. My eyes close and I swallow the lump in my throat.

What would be bad about that scenario?

No, I caution myself. I need to play it cool.

"Do you like me?" he asks, his eyebrows raised high. "Maybe just a little?" He holds his index finger and thumb close together.

I don't answer. I remain silent because I'm still fighting the urge to scream with excitement.

"Maybe like is too strong a word." He rubs his fingers over his chin. "Do you not hate me?" He stares down at me with an expression similar to a puppy waiting for attention.

A giggle I can't contain any longer bursts out of me. "I like you," I say, easing his concern.

"You do?" he questions with narrowed eyes. "Because I've got to be honest with you Harlow, you confuse the fuck out of me." His fingers gently wrap around my upper arms, pulling me closer. "Half the time I can't tell if you like me or despise me."

Placing my hands on his hips, I hook my thumbs through his belt loops. "Kiss me," I say, staring up into his surprised blue eyes. I don't need to ask again. His mouth swoops down, his tongue slips inside seeking mine. His fingers bury in my hair, holding my head in place as his kiss steals my breath from me. It steals all ability for clear thinking and if I'm not careful Brady Lincoln could easily steal my heart too.

My hands slide up his rock-hard body before I use the heels of my palms to push on his chest ending our connection. I wanted his lips on mine, but now that they were, I'm scared. I already feel more for him than I want to. Allowing myself to sink deeper into whatever this is could be a big mistake.

He pulls away, closely studying me. "Everything okay, kitten?"

"Yeah, I just need some time," I answer honestly. There's no sense in sugar coating it. Not to mention, I forgot we were standing in the middle of the kitchen with a table full of spectators. I peek around Brady's shoulder and find a few of the girls watching with scowls on their faces. I'm thankful his broad-shouldered frame blocked the front row view of our kiss. They can only speculate about what we were doing.

He takes my hand, lifts it to his lips and places a kiss on the back. His warm gentle touch sends a signal directly to my heart. It's such a sweet gesture and a massive contradiction to who I've perceived Brady to be for the past year. It makes my chest tighten with all the emotions he stirs up in me. Every wall I've surrounded myself with, he's chipping away at. He's causing cracks in my ivory tower and soon it will all come crashing down. Whether it's with a positive result or a devastating one remains to be seen. Only time will tell. One thing's for sure, I'm helpless to stop him.

He keeps hold of my hand. "Come on. I want to introduce you to some more friends of mine." We walk side by side across the kitchen. I can't avoid the temptation of glancing at the girls seated around the table. All eyes are narrowed on Brady and me. The malice in their stares has my stomach sinking with nerves. I don't want them to notice me. I'm happy flying under the radar.

I breathe a sigh of relief when we leave the kitchen, but it only lasts for a short moment. As soon as I gaze around the room I realize all eyes are on us and the fact he's holding my hand isn't going unnoticed. Tugging on our connection I try to pull from his grasp, but he has a firm hold on me.

"Why are you pulling away?" he asks as we head toward a group of people directly across the room.

"Everyone's looking at us," I answer.

He smirks when his eyes meet mine. "Let them look. Who cares?" He raises our joined hands, kissing the back of mine. It's just as sweet the second time around.

He's unaffected by all the eyeballs aimed our way. He's always the center of attention wherever he goes on campus. This moment is no different than any other day in the life of Brady Lincoln.

I don't know if I can ever get used to the baggage being with him is sure to bring. Just thinking about it makes me anxious.

"Relax, kitten. It's just a party." He reassuringly squeezes my hand.

"Why do you call me kitten?" I question. I've been meaning to ask, but being around him is distracting and he has a way of making me forget about everything else.

"You reminded me of a kitten the first night we met. You were cute and tiny, but your words were like sharp little claws digging into my skin."

"Wow, that's kind of sweet," I say, surprised at his words.

He winks, leading me toward a good-looking guy with dark brown hair. When he turns our way, I notice his hazel eyes and white smile.

"Hey Brady. Who's this gorgeous creature with you?" he asks gesturing at me, a grin on his handsome face.

I flush at his complimentary words and instantly like him. And it's not because he called me gorgeous - although it didn't hurt.

Brady releases my hand, wrapping an arm around my shoulders. "This is Harlow," he introduces me. He gestures at the hazel eyed hottie, "this is Nick."

I smile and we exchange hellos.

"Nick is my other roommate," Brady informs me. "He's the slob out of the three of us. Zeke and I are constantly picking up his shit."

Nick doesn't deny Brady's claims or look remotely guilty about being called out. His posture is relaxed and he has a beer clasped in his left hand. "Why would I clean when you two take care of it for me?" he asks with a mischievous glint in his eyes. "There's no shame in my game." He shrugs and takes a long pull from his bottle.

I giggle and take in Brady's exasperated expression.

He shakes his head. "Can you believe this fucker? It's a good thing he's got skills on the field or we'd be tempted to kick his slovenly ass out."

"That's not the only place I have skills," he interjects with a smirk and polishes his fingernails on his puffed-out chest.

I giggle at his bad joke.

"Sure dude." Brady slaps him twice on the side of his arm. He turns to me with a cocked eyebrow. "Did I forget to mention he's a legend in his own mind?"

"Hey, if I'm not a legend in my own mind then why would anyone else think I'm one?" he asks with complete conviction, as if his words impart some great wisdom, instead of only confusing the listener.

I snort at his logic.

Brady grins, casting his blues in my direction. "You believe this guy?" He gestures toward him with his head.

I tap my finger on my lips. "I think I'm beginning to see why you guys are friends."

"What?" Brady's hand goes to his chest as if my words offend him.

I giggle. "I rest my case."

He turns me in his arms, pulling me close, then kisses me on my forehead. It's so spontaneous, it takes me by surprise. It's the little gestures that get to me every time.

"I love your laugh. And it's even better when I'm the reason for it."

I place my hands on his upper arms. The solid muscles beneath my fingers don't escape me, but right now I'm more interested in Brady the man, not the shape of his body. It was much easier to think of him as a shallow jock with no redeeming qualities. Now, I know that's not true. I haven't even scratched the surface of whom Brady really is.

"I need to use the bathroom. Which direction is it?" I ask, craving some distance between these conflicting emotions.

He spins me around, my back to the solid strength of his chest, his hands on my shoulders. He leans down, placing his lips next to my ear. "It's right down the hallway, last door on the right."

"Thanks," I say, walking forward out of his grasp. As I round the corner I slam into someone. Their drink spills all over me, drenching my chest.

"Aah," I cry out as the icy temperature of the liquid seeps through my sweater and makes contact with my skin.

"Oh, sorry." She giggles.

My head lifts and I recognize her as one of the girls who was playing strip poker in the kitchen. Judging from the way she gave me the stink eye earlier, I start to wonder if this was an accident at all. If I was into betting I'd say probably not and I'd most likely win a bundle. Girls can be so horrible to each other. This is a perfect example of why I only hang out with Raine.

"Not a big deal," I say maneuvering around her. I refuse to let her see me upset by what she did.

"Harlow," she calls my name.

I freeze in place; my eyes squeeze shut for a moment. *How the hell does she know my name?* Spinning around to face her once more, I relax my features. "Yes?"

"You seem like a nice girl and nice girls should stay away from Brady Lincoln. Unless you're happy being one of many."

Pressing my lips together, I nod my head. "Good to know. Thanks for the warning." I take a step backward and then pivot around, walking toward the bathroom as fast as I can. It's vacant, thank god. I can't lock myself in there fast enough and once I do the tears start to flow. I'm not even sure why I'm crying. Maybe it's the wet sweater or maybe it's the reminder I was just given this is Brady's scene, not mine.

Why am I even here?

Staring at my reflection in the mirror I see a girl who has no business being at this party. And there's no one to blame but myself. I let him bring me - let him weaken my resolve with his charm.

Ripping the hand towel from the rack, I press it against my black sweater and do my best to soak up the sticky brown liquid. The thick wet material feels horrible touching my skin; I want to strip it right off. There's no way I can remain here now. I'll be glad to get home and shower this night away.

Leaving the bathroom, I head back toward where I left Brady. As I come around the corner to enter the living room my eyes seek him out. What I see has me stopping short. He's talking to the girl who dumped her drink on me. Not only is he talking to her, he seems pretty fucking happy about it. *What a jerk.*

What am I going to do? My heart races in my chest as my eyes scan the immediate area for anyone I know, but my search is futile. I need to tell Brady I'm ready to leave and all the better if I interrupt their conversation. I don't owe either of these jerks anything.

My stride is fast as I walk in his direction. He notices me when I'm three steps away and smiles throwing me off balance. I stop when I'm next to him and he slips his arm around me.

"Harlow this is Tabby. She's Nick's younger sister and I feel like she's mine too."

My lips spread into a wide smile at his words and the sour look on Tabby's face. "Oh, we've already met, up close and personal on my way to the bathroom."

"Great. I should probably introduce you to some more people."

"Before you do that, I need to talk to you."

He looks concerned as he glances down at me. "Everything okay?" he asks.

My eyes flick in Tabby's direction and then back to him. He picks up on the signal. "Tabby, if you'll excuse us," he says with impeccable manners. Too bad they're wasted on her.

She takes the hint, glaring at me and then walking away without a word.

"What's up?" he asks, pulling me in front of him.

"If you don't mind, I'd like to go home now."

His eyebrows draw together as he frowns. "You're not having a good time?" he questions, his blue eyes delving into mine.

"No, it's not that. Someone spilled their drink on me and I want to get home and change."

He reaches out, brushing his fingers over the material above my chest. "Wet and sticky." He pushes his finger between his lips and then removes it. "But tasty. Let's get you out of here."

We say a few quick goodbyes to some of his friends and then we're on our way. When we reach the sidewalk,

Brady takes my hand as he turns left. "Where are we going? My dorm is in the other direction," I say dragging my feet.

He keeps walking. "I know it is, but my apartment is closer. You can shower, change into one of my shirts and we can continue our date." When he grins down at me, I can't even be annoyed at his bossiness. I swear he could charm the panties off a nun.

How am I supposed to resist him?

His place is only a block from the frat house and I'm glad for the closeness. My damp sweater and the chill of the night air don't mix.

Once we're inside he directs me to his bathroom. "Clean towels are under the sink, there's soap and shampoo in the shower. Give a yell if you need anything, like someone to wash your back or other body parts." He wiggles his eyebrows up and down as he backs out the door. I giggle, pushing it closed in his face.

"Hey, that was cold," he yells from the hallway.

Shaking my head, I smile and begin to remove my clothes. Not only is my sweater a mess but so is my bra. I won't be wearing either again until they've been washed.

I turn on the shower and wait for the water to heat before I step inside. Soaping up my body with one hand, while I hold my hair up with the other is harder than it sounds. A quick rinse is all I dare, knowing Brady could come barging through the door at any moment.

I dry off and wrap the large towel around myself. I'm covered from chest to knees as I leave the bathroom. "Brady," I call his name as I turn left, in the direction of his living room.

"What's up?" he asks from behind me, startling me. I fumble to hang on to my towel. The back slips down dangerously close to exposing my ass for his view. Keeping my back to him, I secure the towel around myself before turning around.

His eyes slowly rake over my body. I can see the desire he feels for me and it's thrilling and intimidating at the same time. "I," my voice cracks. Clearing my throat, I continue. "I need to borrow a shirt."

My breath halts as he stalks toward me - he really walks toward me, but it feels as though I'm his prey and he's closing in fast. He stops when we're toe to toe, handing me the gray t-shirt he's holding in his hand. I never even noticed he had it. I was too wrapped up in the magnetism of his blue eyes. Once they lock on mine, I can't escape.

"Here you go," he says, his voice husky. I know he's as affected by my nearness as I am by his. Our hands brush as I take the folded garment from him. My eyes flash up to meet his and open wide in shock just before he crashes our lips together. At the first touch of his tongue my lids close and I surrender to the moment. There's nowhere I'd rather be, no matter how hard it is for me to admit this. The shirt falls to the floor forgotten as I sink my fingers into the back of his neck and hold my towel with my other hand.

He scoops me up, large hands gripping my ass and my legs wrap around his hips. My bare pussy is pressed against the fly of his jeans as he spins us around toward his bedroom. I lose track of everything but his tongue and the sensual way it moves around mine. He gently lowers me to the mattress, our mouths busy devouring each other. When his hands move between us to slowly spread the towel apart, he pulls his lips from mine and watches, eyes drinking in every inch of my skin as it's bared to him.

"Fuck, you're perfect." The admiration in his tone makes my stomach flutter excitedly. I can't believe I'm lying here naked on Brady Lincoln's bed like it's an everyday occurrence.

His hands cup my breasts and his thumbs rub over both nipples. A moan I can't hold in escapes me. He smiles as he lowers his mouth and pauses when his lips hover over me. "I'm going to make you moan a lot more, Harlow."

His warm breath fans over my nipple. I want his mouth on me now.

"Don't fucking hold them in. I want to hear how good I make you feel." His tongue circles around the edge of my nipple, before passing over the tip. He sucks the pink flesh between his lips and another moan escapes me.

"That's my girl. Give it to me," he growls as he moves to the other side. This time he captures my nipple in his mouth sucking and biting until I think I might go mad. My fingers dig into his scalp, caught between the urge to push him away or pull him closer. My nipple slips from his lips as he trails soft wet kisses down my stomach. He slowly moves lower, teasing me. His lips meander one way before moving in another direction. I know what the destination will be; I just want him to take the fastest route possible.

The shortest distance between two points is a straight line. *Why is he torturing me?*

"Please," I whisper. My hands pressing on the top of his head.

He chuckles against my belly button then runs his nose over the small dip. "Do you want my mouth on your pussy?" He rests his chin on my mound, waiting for me to answer.

"Yes," I sigh. "Please."

He smiles reminiscent of a shark. My head falls back as his tongue licks from my ass to my clit. *Oh god.* He teases my entrance with his tongue and then dips inside to wiggle in the best way possible.

My fingers tug on his hair hard as he sucks my clit between his lips using his tongue to pulse against it. Two large fingers curl inside my pussy pressing exactly how I want them to. My hips move, rocking against his hand and mouth. I can't hold still as I feel my orgasm building.

He growls against my clit like he can't get enough of me. His mouth stays locked on me as my orgasm hits me hard, making my legs shake. My whole-body trembles and it leaves me weak and satisfied. He feasts on me, licking up all traces of my release.

"Fuck, you taste so good," he says crawling up between my legs to hover over me. He smiles down at me. His lips are still shiny from my pussy. He notices me staring and wipes his mouth on his sleeve.

"I could do this all night."

CHAPTER TEN

BRADY

When I tell Harlow I could do this all night, I'm not joking. Making her come was the hottest thing I've ever done and I can't wait to repeat it. But for now, I'll be happy just to get her to spend the night with me.

Standing up, I strip off my shirt and remove my pants and socks. Leaving on my black boxer briefs, I climb into the bed next to her and pull her onto my chest. "Let's go to sleep, kitten. I'm tired," I say, combing my fingers through the long dark strands and enjoying the way their softness trails over my hand.

"I should go home," she murmurs.

"No, you shouldn't. You're staying here with me." I kiss the top of her head. "I'm not letting you leave."

"If you insist," she says and then yawns.

Tightening my arms around her a feeling of contentment washes over me. Smiling, I close my eyes and fall asleep, holding the girl I'm crazy about.

Harlow. She's the first thought in my mind as I begin to stir from my sleep. Smiling, I think about how last night ended and I'm hopeful we can continue this morning. Reaching out without opening my eyes, my hand lands on a bare mattress. My eyes fly open and scan the other side of my king size bed. She's not here. *Fuck.*

Rolling onto my back, I stare up at the white ceiling. *What does her sneaking out mean for us?* I hope she's not regretting what happened last night. I know I'm not.

Just as I've resigned myself I might as well go back to sleep I hear her giggle. Tuning my ears into the sounds around me, I hear Nick's deep laugh join hers. Oh hell no. He can find his own girl.

Jumping out of bed, I grab a pair of basketball shorts from the top of my bureau and pull them up. Slipping a clean t-shirt on, I run my fingers through my hair and make my way to the kitchen. Pausing, I lean against the edge of the doorway with my arms crossed over my chest and watch Harlow. She's frying bacon in a pan on the stove and Nick is sitting on the other side of the butcher-block island, facing her. He has a cup of coffee clenched in both hands and his dark hair is sticking straight up. He must've gotten pretty banged up last night because he looks hungover.

She's still wearing my t-shirt, but her tight fitting jeans are back on. I'd love to see her standing there in nothing but my shirt, but not while Nick is here. The thought of him seeing her like that angers me. She brings out a jealous side of me I never knew existed. I'm not sure how I feel about it.

"Dude, you don't really think that Star Trek The Next Generation is better than Battlestar Galactica. Tell me you're pulling my leg."

"I'm serious. How can you not be a Star Trek fan?" He runs a hand back and forth over his forehead as if he's in pain.

She points the fork in her hand at him. "You should be ashamed. Battlestar Galactica is the greatest sci-fi show ever. Admiral Adama is the best. He could kick Captain Picard's ass, even on a bad day."

"I'm sticking with Jean-Luc. Star Trek is a classic. And you can't beat the classics."

She shakes her head as she plates the bacon. "I can't believe I thought you were Brady's cool friend." She casts a smirk over her shoulder at him.

"You thought I was the cool friend?" he questions with a grin.

Nodding, she spins to face him.

"You're right. I'm way cooler than Zeke. He used to be different before he was with Claire. Now he's afraid to breathe too loud. She wears the pants in their relationship."

Stepping forward into the room, I make my presence known. "Be nice," I caution. "She makes him happy. Even if he has turned into a complete pussy since they've been together." Nick and I chuckle as we bump fists.

"Are you guys joking or has he really?" Harlow questions.

"He's definitely changed, but he's still a great guy. We just like to give him shit about handing his balls over to Claire," I say as I walk over to her. Leaning down, I kiss the top of her head. "Good morning."

Her beautiful face tips up as she smiles at me. "Morning. I hope you like bacon. I fried up the whole package."

"I love it." Reaching behind her I steal a piece from the large pile on the white plate and shove it in my mouth. It's cooked perfectly. Moaning as I chew, I realize this is just another plus about Harlow. I can add *cooks bacon just the way I like* to the list of pros about her. No one should underestimate the importance of bacon in their lives. *It matters.*

"What else are you making for breakfast?" I ask rubbing my hands together. "I usually only make myself a protein shake. This is awesome."

"The ladies don't usually get to stay until morning," Nick blurts out.

I can feel Harlow's eyes burning into the side of my cheek as my eyes narrow while I give him a shut the fuck up glare. *Don't help me any dude.* Fuck. When I glance in her direction she's cracking eggs into the frying pan.

"It's not like girls come back here very often," I say trying to downplay the situation.

"No, we usually fuck them at their places," Nick interjects to clarify.

Taking a deep breath, I remind myself to calm down. I'm about to shove my fist in his mouth and rip out his tongue so he can't dig the hole any deeper than he already has.

"Relax. It's not like I thought you were a virgin, Brady." She rolls her eyes.

Nick barks out a laugh. "That ship sailed a long time ago, like seven years to be exact."

I'm going to knock this motherfucker out in a minute. He's seriously pissing me off. "Nick, don't you have some place to be?" I question, my teeth clenched. *Take the hint motherfucker.*

"No, I don't actually. And even if I did, there's no way I'm leaving without this home cooked breakfast. This beats one of your shit tasting protein shakes any day."

"Well, if you want any teeth left to chew with, then I suggest you shut your big fucking trap."

"So much anger, dude," Nick says his hands held palms up. "Relax. You need to get laid. Harlow, can you help him out?"

She doesn't react to his words. "The verdict is still out. I'm not making any promises," she replies as she cooks the scrambled eggs.

I wrap my arm around her and give her a brief, reassuring squeeze. I want her to know I'm into her for more than the sex. Although when the two of us are finally together, we might burn the building down with how scorching hot it's going to be.

When we're all seated at the island, Harlow and I on one side and Nick on the other the conversation lulls. We're all too busy digging into the fluffy eggs and crunchy bacon she prepared for us. I can't remember the last time I had a big breakfast like this. I think it was during this past summer when I was home with my mom.

"Thanks for cooking all this food. It's the best thing I've eaten since…" My voice trails off as I lean toward her, adding the words I left off. "Late last night," I whisper in her ear.

She drops her head forward, mouth pressed together in a close-lipped smile. "Brady," she mumbles as her cheeks flush pink.

"I'm not going to apologize for being honest." I run my nose along the sensitive skin just behind her ear. She shivers. "I can't wait to bury my tongue in your delectable pussy again. I may never stop."

She closes her eyes and bites on her bottom lip. I can tell my words are affecting her and it's more than embarrassment at my honesty. She likes what I'm saying. She's just not used to someone speaking to her this way. I've never said these things to anyone before. I've never felt this strongly for one person and frankly, I never thought I would. Now that I know she's what I want, I'm not letting her slip through my fingers no matter how slippery she might try to be.

I walk her home when it's early afternoon. Her stained clothes from last night are in a plastic bag I'm carrying. The temperature is cooler today than it has been. I made her put on one of my thick BU hoodies and a knit cap of mine. She looks sexy wearing my clothes.

I tried to get her to stay at my apartment for the remainder of the day, but she insisted she had a lot of studying to do. School is important to her and I would never interfere.

As we make the ten-minute walk to her dorm, I hold her hand the entire way. I like the way her palm feels resting against mine and it goes way beyond sexual attraction. The smallest touch from her makes me feel things I've never experienced before. Just looking at someone has never made my chest feel weak or my heart pound. It's new to me and I'm not sure I like it. But I know I like her so I'll take the good, the bad and the different.

Lost in our own thoughts, both of us are silent. We reach her dorm too soon and I'm not ready to say goodbye. "When am I going to get to see you again?" I question as I tug on her hand, moving her in front of me.

She stares up at me, her gray eyes bright in the afternoon sun. "I'm not sure what my schedule is like this week."

"We can eat lunch together at least." My hands move up to rest on her shoulders, holding her in place. "Let's meet tomorrow at noon in the food court." Staring down into her eyes, I hold my breath and will her to say yes.

"Sure, I can be there," she says. Her lips curve into a smile and I know I'm going to kiss the fuck out of her right now. There's no way to avoid it. Dropping down, I slide my hands in her hair, covering her mouth with mine. Our cold lips quickly warm up and so do the rest of our body parts. Her tongue dancing around mine has my blood roaring through my veins and my heart thumping in my ears. I want to carry her back to my apartment and finish what we started last night. I want to, but I know I must move slow with her. One wrong move and she'll push me completely out of the picture. Not knowing where I stand with a girl is not something I'm familiar with. They all love me. Except for Harlow. I'm not sure how she feels about me from one moment to the next and I don't think she knows either. I need to show her that she wants me in her life.

Pulling my mouth from hers, I rest my forehead on hers. "I had a great time with you last night and this morning. I'm going to miss you."

"I had fun too."

I kiss the tip of her nose and then release my hold, letting my hands fall away. She hesitatingly takes a step backward and then another.

I smile, lifting my chin, gesturing for her to go. "Get inside before you freeze. I'll see you tomorrow at noon."

She nods. "See ya then," she says, pivoting to walk away from me. My eyes lock on her retreating form, watching every step she takes until with a smile and a final wave of her hand, she disappears inside the building.

CHAPTER ELEVEN

HARLOW

"Well, well, well. Look who's doing the walk of shame," Raine says as I walk inside our dorm room.

I spin around and lean back against the inside of the door. I can't keep the smile off my face. It stretches from cheek to cheek, so wide and full it makes my eyes squint. "You're never going to believe who I spent the night with." The words leave me in a jumbled rush of excitement. Now that I'm back in my own space the magnitude of what happened last night is sinking in.

"Brady?" Raine questions, looking at the sweatshirt I'm still wearing, emblazoned with his number.

"What gave it away?" I joke. Stepping away from the door, I make my way over to my bed. Kicking my shoes off, I sink down on my mattress lost in a lust filled haze of Brady Lincoln.

It's such a relief to be home and not keep my defenses up. It's a constant struggle when I'm with him. I want to dive head first into whatever is developing between us, but my self-preservation instincts kick in.

Tugging off his black knit cap I'm still wearing, I fall to my back with a large sigh. "I really like him, Raine. What am I going to do?"

"Keep liking him?"

Raising my head, I roll my eyes at her. "If only it were easy. A little cut and dried would be awesome right now. It's not like that, though. There are so many factors that'll work against us if I allow this to go on anymore."

"How do you know? Maybe you should try to roll with it and see what happens."

Closing my eyes, I picture Brady smiling at me and I know I should let this play out however it will. At least then I'll know I didn't let fear stop me. Giving us a chance is a risk, but I'm already crazy about him at this point. I can't play it safe any longer. Tomorrow at lunch I'm going to tell him how I feel. *Maybe.*

Adjusting the strap of my messenger bag higher on my shoulder, I navigate my way down the sidewalk. Hurrying from one class to another is never fun, and today the air has an extra crispness to it, making my lungs ache and my cheeks burn. I shove my phone into the side pocket of my coat, annoyed I'm waiting to hear from Brady. He usually says good morning around this time. I know we already have plans to eat lunch together, but I was looking forward to his sweet message.

Glancing around, I search the immediate area for a sign of him. We don't have many classes near each other, but right now his lecture is one building over from the one my next class is in. Just as I'm about to give up hope I notice him talking to a redhead. Her back is to me and I can't see who she is but they seem familiar judging by his wide smile. My hand covers my mouth smothering the gasp before it can escape while I watch them share a hug. Shaking my head, I run up the stairs and into the building. I can't watch any longer.

Brady knows a lot of girls. It was probably just someone saying hello. I caution myself not to overreact. I'll just keep my eyes open for other signs he's not through with his playboy ways.

My stomach is tied in nervous knots as I arrive at the food court right on time. I haven't felt well since this morning when I saw him with his arms wrapped around some other girl. *Don't think about it.* My eyes scan the area for a sign of Brady's dark blonde hair or tall stature, but I don't see him anywhere. Expelling a large sigh, I walk across the tiled floor to the salad bar.

Reaching for a plate, a deep voice in my ear startles me. "Hey beautiful."

My head snaps over my shoulder to catch my first glimpse of Brady. His grin is infectious and makes me smile back.

"Hey, I thought maybe you were standing me up." I turn to face him and notice the large pizza box from Gino's in his hands. My eyes go wide and my mouth waters in anticipation of the first taste. "You brought me lunch?"

"I did. Let's go find a table. Grab some plates and napkins for us, if you don't mind."

Scooping up both items, I follow him to a table in the right back corner of the food court. This is the perfect spot to give us some privacy. I assume he did this for me and I really appreciate the gesture.

He sets the box down in the middle of the round table then pulls my chair out for me.

"Thank you for choosing this corner. It was really thoughtful of you to keep me away from all the prying eyes."

"What makes you think it was that noble of a gesture?" he asks, then leans over toward me. "Maybe, I just wanted some privacy so I can steal a kiss or two from my girl." He winks at me.

My eyes lock with his. "Your girl, huh? Is that what I am?" I lick my suddenly dry lips and wait for his answer.

"That depends on you. I want you to be my girl." He runs the back of his fingers down my cheek. His touch is gentle and caring. "Hell, I already think of you as mine. What do you say? Put me out of my misery and say you'll give us a chance. I want to take you out whenever I can."

"I've been thinking about this a lot. I didn't want to rush a decision and then regret it later." Pausing, I stare into his deep blue eyes and pray I'm not making a bad decision, especially after what I saw this morning. But this doesn't feel like a mistake. We don't feel like a mistake, but only time will tell. His eyebrows draw together as he waits for my answer. "Yes, I want to be your girl."

He grins at my words and then pulls me out of my chair and into his lap. "Give me those sweet lips. I can't wait any longer to kiss you," he says, his hands tightening on my hips.

Wrapping my arms around his neck, I press my lips to his. His hands move up to cup my cheeks, holding me in place as his tongue slowly dances with mine.

"Is this a Gino's pizza?" Nick's voice interrupts us.

Brady rests his forehead against mine. "So much for privacy. We better eat something before Nick steals it all."

"Hey, I resent that," Nick replies, staring pointedly at Brady, a large slice of pizza already in his hand. I giggle, reaching into the box for a slice of my own. Bringing it to my lips I take a bite and then hold it in front of Brady. He tears a large chunk off with his teeth and we both groan as we chew.

"I had convinced myself their pizza couldn't possibly be as good as I remembered, but it's even better." Taking another bite, I hold it out for him to do the same. We share the rest of the piece and when I choose another I tell him, "you're on your own now. This one is all mine."

He lifts me from his lap, placing me in my own chair. "So that's how it's going to be?" he says with a smirk and reaches into the box for his own slice. Nick has already made short work of two pieces. Brady raises a brow at him. "Dude, get lost. I'm trying to eat lunch with my girl."

"Fuck off. You should know by now if you bring Gino's pizza I'm close behind. If you bring it, he will follow."

I giggle at his answer. He's entertaining for sure.

"Did you catch my movie reference?" Nick asks me.

I nod. "I did. Field of Dreams, it's a great movie. I've watched it many times with my dad." Brady rubs his palm over my back at the mention of my father.

Nick looks at me with an expression of awe on his face before his eyes slide over to Brady. "Dude, you have the perfect girl for me." He glances in my direction.

Brady scowls. "The hell I do. Find your own girl." He wraps his arm around my shoulder, his fingertips lightly skimming up and down my arm.

Nick places his hand over his heart. "Harlow, you and I were meant to be. You love sci-fi and Field of Dreams, come on. I'll even watch Battlestar Galactica with you. I doubt this guy will." He lifts his chin in Brady's direction.

Brady chuckles. "Don't spout off bullshit about what I will or won't do. I get it, you're kicking yourself because I have such great taste. I'm sure you won't be the only one."

"Okay, we'll see how long this lasts," Nick mentions, his skepticism more than apparent.

Brady meets his stare, his expression serious. "Don't be an asshole."

"I'm not. I'm just being optimistically skeptical." Nick shakes his head.

"What the fuck does that even mean?" Brady questions.

Nick holds up his hands. "It means I'm not sure how long Harlow will put up with you, but I'm thinking positive."

"So, it's like that?" Brady asks.

"Dude, don't be so sensitive. I hope you're happy forever and ever," he mocks, his hand over his heart

"Isn't it time for you to beat it? I want to spend some time with Harlow," Brady grumbles

"Harlow, it was nice seeing you again. I'm going to make myself scarce now." He deftly grabs one more slice of pizza, winking at me. I giggle and turn my head to look up at Brady. Resting my chin on his arm, I study the angles of his face. His nose is straight with a slight bump in the bridge and his lips are masculine in shape. Feeling the heat of my gaze, he turns his head to glance down at me. Leaning down he brushes his lips against mine. "Are you sure you still want to be my girl? I might need to lock you away to get any time alone with you."

"I'm sure."

The stadium seats are cold underneath me. The chilly November temperatures of this Friday night, make it difficult to sit still and watch the rest of the football game. Raine and I are huddled together seeking any warmth we can find underneath a fleece blanket. Thank god the people next to us had an extra one. We'd be frozen solid by now without it. My fingers are numb even with the thick knit gloves I'm wearing. Earmuffs weren't enough protection and I had to add the black knit cap of Brady's I've yet to return. I may be holding on to it on purpose. His masculine scent is all over it and sniffing it at different points this week helped me get through the past four days. I still can't believe I did that.

It's been four long days since I've seen Brady. He's been busy with football practices and gym time, not to mention he still has to attend his classes.

My own schoolwork has been keeping me occupied and the one night I could've spent some time with him, I had to meet my stepmother Cindy. She was here for the day and wouldn't tell me why, but she wanted to check in on me. We went to dinner at some restaurant that screamed pretentious and snobbish, just the kind of place she prefers.

I wish I could've taken her to Gino's, but it's not someplace she'd like. She would've curled her bright pink lipstick coated upper lip at me and I'd have never heard the end of it. A lecture about how I won't be thin forever would've followed.

As it was, I had to listen to how she's in the gym four days a week to keep her body fit. It was all I could do to not roll my eyes and I had to bite my lip on more than one occasion. She does look great for her age, but what good is that when her personality is so lacking. I'm sure there are some guys who'd be happy to have her on their arm or in their bed, but those aren't the ones who are good for the long haul. I want someone who's there for better or worse and not just because I'd make good eye candy.

Her shortage of motherly concern used to make me sad, but now I've come to accept she gives me all she's capable of.

The cheers of the crowd are a welcome interruption from thoughts of my stepmother and the dinner we shared. "What happened?" I ask Raine.

"Aren't we watching the same game?" she asks her voice filled with sarcasm.

"Yeah, sorry. Just thinking about dinner with my mother the other night."

"Gross, why would you willingly think about her?"

"I know. It was a momentary lapse in sanity. So what did I miss?" My eyes greedily seek out Brady on the field. I need to focus on the good in my life, not the things I've no control over.

"They got the first down they needed," Raine informs me.

I watch the remaining two minutes of the game as Brady leads his team down the field to score, reminiscent of his favorite quarterback Tom Brady. I jump up and down and cheer, happy he won, but in the back of my mind I'm dreading going to another party.

Raine and I head outside to wait by Brady's Tahoe. She has plans with Cameron again. We haven't really discussed what's going on with them. She knows I'm not a fan of his. Any guy who grabs the ass of a girl he doesn't know is a dickhead and not worth her time. She doesn't see it that way. She's enamored with his social status and big dick - her words, not mine.

"Are you going to do the dirty deed with Brady tonight?" Raine asks, a mischievous expression on her face.

"What?" I ask with a laugh.

"Are you going to bump uglies? Bang? Fuck? Slam? Smash? Do the deed? Tickle his pickle? Ride the baloney pony?" She laughs when she says the last one and I join in.

"That's a horrible way to refer to it and possibly the least sexy way also," I inform her.

"I'm pretty sure I can come up with worse. How much time do I have?"

I snort at her answer.

"What's all the commotion about over here?" Brady asks as he and Cameron walk up to us. Raine practically skips over to stand beside Cameron.

I smile up at him. "Nothing we can tell you about."

He leans down brushing a quick kiss over my lips.

"We'll see you later, right?" Cameron questions Brady.

"I'm not sure. Great game though, man." They bump fists.

Raine smiles and waves her fingers as she turns to walk away with Cameron, his arm wrapped around her shoulders.

Grabbing my hip with one hand, Brady leans down, claiming my attention. He brushes his nose along mine before skimming over my cheek. His lips close around my earlobe and then are replaced by his teeth as he gently tugs before releasing it. "I'm glad you came to watch me." His breath is warm in my ear and makes me shiver. His lips hover over my cheek before he kisses my forehead. "How did you like the game?" he asks.

"It was awesome. You played great. My favorite play was when you rushed twelve yards for that first down," I say, wrapping my arms around his waist, squeezing him tight. His hand slides from my hip around my back to rest at the top of one ass cheek.

"Did I ever tell you how much it turns me on when you talk about football?" He drops the duffel bag to the ground, splaying the fingers of his other hand out in the middle of my back. I rise up on my toes as his lips come down to claim mine with a sense of urgency. Our tongues hungrily explore and I lose track of everything, but the warm, wet strokes and the press of our bodies against one another. The beep of a car alarm nearby brings me back to the present and I pull my mouth from his.

His eyes are heated as they stare down into mine. "Let's get out of here. If it's okay with you I'd like to skip the party tonight." His hand reaches out, his fingers caress along the curve of my jaw, and then his thumb traces over my bottom lip. "I'd like to spend some time alone with you."

"I'd like that too," I reply, relieved I won't be on display. I wasn't looking forward to another party, but of course, I'd tough it out for him.

His Tahoe is spacious but it only takes a few minutes before the heat is kicking in. Groaning, I lean my head back into the soft seat. "I was so chilled, I never thought I'd be warm again."

Brady smiles. His eyes briefly flick to me before returning to the road. "I don't even feel the cold when I'm playing."

"I know, I couldn't believe you were out there in short sleeves. Watching made me even colder."

"Nice hat by the way," he says with a flash of his white teeth.

"I...thanks." I flush and stumble to find the words.

"I like you in my clothes." His words surprise and reassure me.

"Good because I might never give it back."

Once we're at his apartment, I hang my jacket up on an empty hook next to the vest he wore the other night and tuck the earmuffs, hat and gloves in the side pockets.

"I'm going to see what I can scrounge up for us to eat. I'm always starving after a game. Make yourself at home." Brushing my bangs to the side, I watch him walk away. I let my eyes take him in from the top of his hair, down to his shoulders which seem broader than ever in the black henley he has on. My gaze wanders down to his lean hips and the way his jeans snuggly fit his ass. His legs are long and muscular from all his training. I know how powerful they are after watching him play. He's limber and agile on the field and I can't help but wonder what it would be like to have sex with him.

As if he can feel me ogling him, he glances over his shoulder at me. He flashes me a wink letting me know I've been caught checking him out.

Oh well. It's not like he doesn't know he's hot. Every girl on campus wants him. Blowing out a large sigh, I walk toward his living room. I don't want to think about Brady and all the girls who've come before me - literally. It turns my stomach to think of how many there could be. Has he reached triple digits? Quadruple?

Sinking down onto the couch, the disturbing path my thoughts have taken has me feeling less enthused about being here.

"I hope you like chicken salad" he says, placing a large oval plate in the center of the coffee table. There are four wraps and a pile of potato chips in the middle. "I need to eat a lot after I play," he explains, standing in front of me. "What can I get you to drink? Water? Beer?"

"I'll take a beer thanks." *You only live once.* And if this night ends where I think it might - where I hope it will; I'll need all the help I can get.

He returns, handing me a beer, before taking a seat next to me with a bottle of his own in hand. Raising it, my lips immediately close around the glass rim as I take a large sip.

"Don't be shy. Dig in." He leans forward choosing one of the wraps and then places a napkin on his thigh before adding a handful of chips on top.

Reaching over, I grab a few chips from his pile and laugh at his expression of feigned anger as I push one between my lips.

He takes a large bite of the wrap and then holds it in front of my mouth. Leaning forward, I do as he wants. Chewing it, I'm pleasantly surprised by how good it is.

"Come on, you can do better than that," he encourages me as he holds the roll up in front of me again. This time I take a larger bite and moan as the flavors hit my taste buds.

I crunch through the rest of the salty and somewhat greasy chips and suck the residue from my fingers before I realize Brady is watching. Smiling, I glance at him to apologize for my lack of manners when I find him staring ferally at me. The heat in his gaze has liquid pooling between my thighs. I've never had anyone look at me with such intensity. I like it. I like it too much. I nervously gulp down some more of my beer.

He smiles and pushes the rest of the wrap into his mouth, followed by the remainder of chips. I contemplatively sip my beer, studying him. I don't know why anything to do with him surprises me at this point, but Brady knowing his way around the kitchen does. I know he can man a blender and make a protein shake, but I didn't think he'd know how to do anything, besides dial for takeout.

I know I need to forget all the bad things I convinced myself were true about him. I'm ashamed I had no concrete evidence to base any of my misconceptions on.

"You're a lot different than I thought you'd be," I say as our eyes connect. "I might've misjudged you without giving you the benefit of the doubt. I owe you an apology," I sheepishly confess.

His hand lands on my knee. "You don't owe me anything, Harlow. You're here now; that's what matters." He runs his fingers up toward mid-thigh and back down to my knee. His simple touch has my stomach fluttering and me craving so much more. "And for the record, I'm glad you're here," he says, his expression earnest.

"So am I." I sip my beer, covertly stealing glances at him beside me. He stirs up feelings inside me I've never experienced before, making me wish for something, but not be able to put my finger on exactly what it is I want. I know I want to kiss him. I want to do so much more, but this is Brady Lincoln. After having some of the hottest girls in our school, my amateur seduction wouldn't be very interesting. I drink down the rest of my beer and place the empty bottle down on the coffee table. Perched on the edge of the couch, I'm lost in indecision. Should I kiss him or not? It's not the kiss itself I'm contemplating. It's everything that comes after because we both know there will be no stopping once we start. There's an energy between us, a low hum below my skin signifying taking things to the next level is inevitable. The attraction between us has been growing for the past few weeks and it's getting too big to contain.

If I was braver I'd crawl into his lap, straddle his muscular thighs and lay a kiss he'd never forget on him. But, I'm not. Instead, I'm going to sit here and try to summon the courage to put myself out there.

His hand closes around my upper arm. "Hey, what are you thinking about?" he questions as he spins me around to face him. I open my mouth to answer when he leans forward, lifting me into his lap. I end up in the very position I was fantasizing about. His large hands on my hips, holding me in place.

"All that football talent and you can read minds too." I shake my head and smile as my fingers grip onto the top of his shoulders.

He raises an eyebrow at me. "Mind reading?" he questions. "I'm not sure I know what you mean."

Instead of answering and clueing him into my insecurities I make the most of the opportunity he gave me by crashing our lips together. He grunts in surprise and then one of his hands slides sensually up my spine to grip the back of my head. His tongue licks at my lips and then he tugs the bottom one between his teeth. The mix of gentle and rough has my panties soaked. He holds me immobile as his mouth ravenously devours mine. It's as if a switch has been flipped and we can't get enough of each other. My breasts are smashed against his chest, my hips rolling and grinding my pussy down onto his hard cock as our kiss continues. We can't get close enough. I've never felt this incredible need for someone before. I can't get enough of the way Brady touches me. His hands are magic on my body.

Tearing my mouth from his, my breaths are rough and labored as I strip my shirt off. His gaze is feral as he studies me in my pink lace bra.

He quickly rises to his feet, with me securely in his grasp. "Our first time together isn't going to be on the couch where anyone can walk in and see us," he tells me as he enters his bedroom with me in his arms. He kicks the door shut behind him and walks with purpose to the foot of his bed. He sets me down on my feet and cups my cheeks with both his palms. "Are you sure you're ready to do this?" he questions, staring deep in my eyes. "I can't take it back once it's done and I don't want you to regret it tomorrow."

The lamp on his desk and the one on his nightstand provide enough light for me to notice the sincerity in his expression. I bite on my bottom lip, fighting the urge to cry happy tears. I can tell by the way he's looking at me he cares deeply for me which is all I need to know.

CHAPTER TWELVE

BRADY

Nodding her head, she says, "yes, I want this to happen." They're the best words I've ever heard. My fingers fly to undo the button on her jeans and then quickly pull down the zipper. The sound of the metal teeth sliding against each other is an erotic buzz in the silence of the room. I'm not playing around. She needs to be mine now, before she changes her mind.

Her hips wiggle side to side as she pushes the tight material down to the floor before kicking it out of the way. The sight of her in only her pink bra and matching panties steals my breath. She's perfect with her delicate curves and full tits.

"You're gorgeous." I shake my head. "I can't believe you're here with me right now." I drop to my knees, ready to worship her body in any way I can. Her large gray eyes are filled with need as she stares down at me. My lips trail down her silky skin to the edge of her panties and my hands slide down to cup her round ass, one cheek to fill each. I nuzzle my nose against her smooth stomach, then along the straight edge of her panties, dragging it down the middle of her mound and over her clit. Burying my face against her lace covered pussy, I inhale her scent. My mouth waters at the thought of tasting her sweet juices again and I know I can't wait any longer.

"Take your bra off," I order before gripping each side of her panties. I slide them down her leanly muscled legs and urge her back onto the end of the bed. She drops her bra to the floor and reclines on her elbows as I tear my shirt over my head. Her eyes slowly appraise every inch of my chest and hard earned six pack. I tug her down the bed by her ankles knocking her flat onto her back and she giggles. Her legs go over my shoulders, my hands cup her ass, lifting her pussy up for my tongue to swipe along her slit. Her giggles turn into moans and gasps as my tongue licks and teases every inch of her pussy.

She tastes even better than I remembered. The way she's gripping my hair and pushing on the back of my head, grinding her clit against my tongue is so fucking hot. I love how she's not afraid to take what she wants.

One of my hands slides from her ass, forward and I sink two fingers into her hot little hole. Fuck. My teeth grind as I curl my fingers inside her. Moaning she rocks against my hand and tongue. Sucking her clit into my mouth I gently rake it between my teeth until she trembles through her orgasm.

Jumping to my feet, I grab the condom from my pocket. I stashed it there earlier hoping we'd end up here, but definitely not counting on it. I tear off my jeans, boxers and socks, throwing each article of clothing down as I remove it.

"Move up to the pillows," I order as I stroke my fist up and down my cock. I don't know if I've ever been this hard in my life. I don't take my eyes off her as she wiggles backward on the bed. The movement has her tits bouncing and I can't wait to see them jiggle from my dick repeatedly thrusting inside her. Tearing open the wrapper, my eyes only leave her to place the condom on the tip. My gaze returns to her as I roll it down my length.

Placing a knee on the bed, I crawl up between her legs, wrapping them around my hips as my cock nudges against her entrance. "I need to be inside you, kitten. I can't fucking wait any longer." Leaning down on my forearms, my hands hold the sides of her head and our gazes lock as I slowly press past her entrance. Staring into each other's eyes like this feels so intimate and different than anything I've ever experienced before.

Goddamn she's so tight, clenching my teeth, I hold still for a moment. This can't be over before it's even begun. I pull back and thrust inside her fully, a large breath expels as I'm seated balls deep inside her for the first time.

Oh fuck. As much as I want to go slow and savor this feeling, my hips move like they have a mind of their own - and maybe they do. My dick seems to be doing all the thinking for me right now. Each thrust is an exquisite torture unlike anything I've ever known. Now that I've had Harlow, I'm never going to let her go. "You feel so fucking good," I growl, then slide a hand down to her hip. My fingers dig into her fair skin as I grip onto her with each thrust of my dick. My other hand clenches her hair, tugging her head back, exposing the delicate skin of her neck for my lips to taste.

With each thrust a sense of urgency builds. My pace increases until I don't know how much longer I can hold on for. I roll over to my back, bringing her with me. My dick remains snug inside her. She's so sexy rocking her hips into mine. "Fuck yeah, ride my cock," I say as I grip her hip in one hand and slip the other one between us to rub her clit with my thumb. She moans at the first touch on her engorged flesh. "You like?" my voice is a husk as it leaves me.

"Yes," she moans. "Don't...stop. It's so...good."

My hips thrust up to meet hers each time she rolls down into me. It's never been like this before. Being with her is fucking phenomenal and she's never doing this again with anyone but me.

Her head tips back lost in the pleasure she's experiencing and her hands move behind her, nails digging into my thighs. Her back is arched, her tits thrusting forward and I know I've never seen anything as beautiful as she is in this moment.

My thumb flicks and circles her clit. "Come on, I know you're close," I coax. My other hand slides up from her hip to the middle of her back. My palm urges her down toward me and she closes the space between us until her lips are on mine and our tongues are colliding. Her hair is draped all over me, a soft dark curtain to enshroud us. This is what I wanted - to be wrapped up in her in every possible way. To be lost in everything she is. She rocks into me once more before she moans into my mouth as she comes. *Fuck.* My hips thrust a few more times, before I shudder and groan through the best orgasm of my life.

She collapses on my chest, her face buried in my neck. Our harsh breaths merge in the silence of the space and my arms close around her. I kiss her head and take in the fragrance of her hair as I hold her close.

After another minute, when we've both calmed down, she raises her head, staring down at me. Our eyes lock and this moment feels special beyond the obvious. It's fateful, like we were destined to get to this point. I can't believe I'm having these thoughts. I never imagined caring about someone with the depth of feelings I have for her.

My hands smooth her hair back from her face before I bury my fingers in her hair. "I'm falling for you, Harlow. Falling so fucking hard and I never want to stop."

She smiles, her lower lip wobbles before she bites on it. The sheen of tears shows in her eyes. "I'm falling for you too," she whispers. "Be careful with my heart, Brady Lincoln."

A single tear trails down her cheek. Wiping it away with my thumb, I smile at her. "I will. Always."

I wake to the sound of a door slamming followed by another one shortly after. What the fuck? Don't my asshole roommates know we're trying to get some sleep. Opening my eyes, I notice the sun peeking in along the edges of the blinds on my windows. It's later than it feels like, but I'm not ready for the real world to intrude.

Harlow's still here - naked in my arms. Last night was the best night of my life and this morning is starting off better than any other.

Burying my face in the softness of her dark tresses on the white pillowcase in front of me, I inhale the floral scent of her shampoo. I could get used to this. I only hope I get the chance.

I've never woken up with someone in my arms before. I don't usually spend the night and I never encourage random hook ups to sleep over. Once we fuck, it's usually, "you can go now or what are you still doing here?"

Harlow begins to stir, sliding her leg along the outside of mine where it's sandwiched between hers. The skin on skin contact has my body responding. As if laying with her in my arms wasn't enough to test my resolve she lets out a sexy little moan and rubs her ass against my cock. I pull my hips back from her, quickly eliminating any more contact with the heart shaped temptation.

She pushes her ass back, narrowly missing my dick. "Where are you?" She groans, reaching her hand back to tug on my thigh. "Come cuddle with me," she whispers.

Sliding my hips forward, I let her feel the full effect of what she does to me. "I was trying to be a gentleman," I say as I press my cock in the middle of her ass.

She presses back into me more. "Who wants a gentleman in bed?" she asks, giggling.

"Be careful what you ask for," I growl in her ear as my chest pushes against her back, rolling her to her stomach. Coming to my knees, I straddle her legs and rub my cock back and forth in the crack of her ass. Fuck. Leaning forward, I press my chest to her back and let my lips enjoy the curve of her ear. She moans.

"Tell me what you need, Harlow. I'll give you anything you desire." My voice is husky with need. If I don't bury myself in her pussy soon, I'm going to come all over her ass.

"I want you," she says.

"You can do better than that, kitten." I slide my cock forward and then back again, pausing near the entrance to her pussy. "Be specific. What do you want me to do to you?"

"I want you to fuck me," she moans, glancing over her shoulder at me. Her eyes are glassy with passion.

Reaching in the nightstand drawer, I grab a condom and my dick is sheathed in record time.

Gripping both her wrists, I stretch her arms out above her head. "Keep your hands here," I order, pressing them flat on the sheets. My fingers then clench into the skin on both of her hips, pulling her to her knees, hips up in the air. Running my cock through her dripping slit, I rub her clit with the head. She moans and bucks her ass back toward me.

"Is this what you want?" I tease her, pressing against her entrance.

"Yes...fuck...yes," she gasps.

My teeth clench as I slowly enter her, taking my time. My hips draw back and move forward at an unhurried pace. Each time going deeper inside her tight pussy. Leaning down, my chest on her back, I clasp my fingers with hers while my lips and tongue taste the skin just below her ear. Using long, slow strokes my eyes close as I get lost in the sensation of her hot wet pussy. For the first time in my life I understand what it means to make love to someone. "You're mine," I growl in her ear. "Tell me you're mine." I thrust deeper. "Tell me," I growl.

"Yes...I'm yours."

Rising to my knees, my hands caress the smoothness of her ass and then dig into the flawless skin of her hips when I pick up the pace of my thrusts. Staring down at how hot my dick looks sliding in and out of her has me ready to come. Reaching one hand around her, I move down to rub her clit.

"Fuck...yes," she moans, her fingers clenching the sheets.

My fingers move quicker, flicking and rubbing in time with my strokes. I will myself to hang on for one more thrust over and over until she finally trembles through her orgasm. Her cunt squeezing my length sends me over the edge and I shudder through my own release.

My head falls back while I fight to catch my breath. My hands move along the graceful curves of her ass and up her back. I drop down, resting my weight on my forearms on either side of her. Kissing the skin beneath her jaw, my lips move up to rest on the bottom of her ear. "Be my girlfriend," I say, the words flying out of me unexpectedly.

Her head spins to cast a glance at me over her shoulder. "What?" she asks. The surprise she's feeling is written all over her face. "I thought I already was."

"I asked you to be my girl and it wasn't the most romantic setting. But right here, right now buried inside you is perfect. Please be my girlfriend?" I ask, nuzzling her cheek with my nose and lips. The more I think about this, the more I realize how much I want her to say yes. I pull out of her and roll to the side so she can do the same. Facing each other, our gazes locked, I ask her again. "Will you please be my girlfriend?" Holding my breath, I wait for her to answer. I'd like to think she's going to say yes, but in all actuality, I don't know what's going to come out of her mouth. She's not like other girls which is one of my favorite things about her, but right now, I wish she was more predictable. Then I wouldn't have this sinking feeling in my stomach waiting for her to reply.

She stares at me for what seems like forever. "I'll be your girlfriend on one condition. You must be faithful to me. If you can't, then tell me upfront and spare me the heartache later."

I grin at her. "Fuck yes, I'll be faithful to you."

"Then it looks like you've got yourself a girlfriend, Brady Lincoln."

The jarring impact of the hard-hit I just took leaves me breathless and the entire crowd gasping. I've been sacked five times in the fourth quarter alone and each time I'm a little slower to get up. This time I'm not sure I'm going to make it up off the field at all. My ribs are screaming and I've just taken my first breath after having the wind knocked out of me. It's not until Zeke holds a hand in front of me that I muster a shallow sigh of relief. Anything more than that has my ribs screaming in pain. I'm no pussy, but I'm not sure how much more of this pummeling I can take. Besides my ribs, my throwing shoulder is killing me. One of the defensive linemen on the other team drilled me into the ground four plays ago and my shoulder took the brunt of our combined weight. Big boy must be close to three hundred pounds and he felt like a ton landing on me. My shoulder is stiff as fuck now, but I'm going to do the best I can. We're going to lose this game. Admitting that is a fucking bitter pill to swallow, but there's no getting around it. We're down by twenty-one points with only two minutes left. I'm good, but I'm not a fucking miracle worker. Even Tom Brady himself couldn't come back from that deficit and lack of time to win.

Our opponents scored on the opening drive and have dominated the entire game. No matter what we've tried we haven't been able to get all components functioning how we need to. We've sucked all around which means we're about to lose our playoff game. Our season is about to be over. *Fuck.*

We manage to add another seven points to the scoreboard, when Nick catches a missile I launched right at his chest. We still lost by fourteen points, but at least we went down fighting.

The mood is somber in the locker room. I grab a quick shower, my mind already thinking of Harlow and how she'll make this loss less painful for me. She's become an important part of my life and I can't imagine being without her.

I don't bother cleaning out my locker like a lot of the guys are. I'll come back tomorrow or the next day and take care of it then. Right now, I just want to see my girl.

My heart races when I first see her. She's standing at the end of the hallway, hands in her coat pockets, staring down at the cement floor. Her expression is pensive. *What is she thinking about?*

She must sense me watching because her eyes rise and immediately lock on me. She wears a hesitant smile on her lips, unsure of what my mood is. I grin back. That was the signal she was waiting for. She flashes me a breathtakingly beautiful smile. My chest aches from all the emotions she makes me feel. One of these days I'll find the courage to say the words she deserves to hear.

CHAPTER THIRTEEN

BRADY

"Are you sure I'm not underdressed?" Harlow asks for the second time this morning.

"No, you look beautiful," I answer honestly as my eyes take her in from head to toe. She has on black pants, a red sweater and her black wool coat. The black boots on her feet are hot. They remind me of a biker chick. Maybe she can wear them later when she rides me. I chuckle to myself.

"Do I even want to know what your laugh is about?" she asks as we walk inside the building where my dad and stepmom live.

Glancing at her I smile. "I'm just picturing you in nothing but your boots."

"Brady." She rolls her eyes.

"Hey, they're hot boots. I'm only human."

She adjusts the strap of her purple backpack on her shoulder and shoots me an exasperated look. "Here, let me take that for you," I say, holding out my hand. She hands it over and says, "thanks." I sling her bag over my left shoulder, along with the black backpack containing my clothes. We're in New York City for the next two days and staying at my dad's. I'm looking forward to showing her around while we're here.

"Mr. Lincoln, it's great to see you. How've you been?" Curtis, the concierge of the building asks as he rushes over to greet us when we come through the door from the private garage.

"Hi, good to see you too, Curtis. I've been great. Can't complain," I answer, wrapping my arm around her shoulders. "This is my girl, Harlow." I gesture to her with my free hand. "We go to school together. Harlow, this is Curtis. He makes sure this place runs ship shape. He keeps everyone in line."

They exchange pleasantries while my eyes reacquaint themselves with the luxurious decor of the lobby. The marble tile floors are shiny and clean. The small groupings of furniture are made from the softest leather and I know how comfortable they are to sink down into. The expansive waterfall feature running the length of the right-side wall took more than a week to construct and cost an ungodly amount of money.

We make our way over toward to the hallway on the left side of the lobby. I tug on Harlow's hand, pulling her along with me when she stops in front of the first bank of elevators. "This way, beautiful," I say as we keep moving forward down the long hall. Her eyes drift to the sedate and expensive artwork along each side wall. The sound of our steps on the marble floors echoes unnaturally loud through the silence. Harlow presses her lips together and tries to creep on her tip toes.

I chuckle at her effort to be quiet. "This place feels like a museum," I say, aiming a reassuring smile at her. "I wish

I could say my dad's apartment will be different, but it's not."

I point at the single elevator in front of us, indicating where we're headed. I swipe the card that gives me access to the private transport for the penthouse apartment where my father and his family live. The inside is covered in a medium toned wood paneling which wraps all the way around the 3 interior walls. The stainless-steel doors make up the fourth and I can see our reflection in them as they close. Harlow looks so tiny standing next to me. Turning, I lean down and kiss the top of her sweet-smelling hair as we begin our ascent.

Her face tips up to look at me. "I love when you do that."

"What? Kiss your head?" I question.

She nods, a soft smile on her face. "My dad used to do that. It reminds me of him, but more than anything it makes me feel like you really care about me."

My fingers clasp her arm spinning her to face me. My other hand falls to her hip as I say, "I do care about you - more than you probably realize." Raking my teeth over my bottom lip, I search for the right words. "Being someone's boyfriend is new to me. I've never been in a relationship before. I'm going to do my best to make you happy, but if there's something you need you're not getting from me…" I pause, raising the hand from her arm up to cup her cheek. "You're going to have to tell me. I don't ever want to make you unhappy." My eyebrows draw downward as I think about the words I'm about to say. "It feels inevitable that I'll disappoint you sooner or later."

Her hands slide up my chest and come to rest on my shoulders. "Don't think like that. I care about you. If you're honest and faithful, we'll be right as rain." Her wide smile dispels any worry I'm feeling.

"Are you nervous to meet my family?"

"No, not really. They're either going to like me or they won't." Her shoulders raise in a quick shrug. "All I can do is be myself and hope for the best."

Leaning down, I brush my lips against hers. "I can't imagine anyone not liking you," I say.

"Right? Only crazy people wouldn't like me."

The elevator comes to a halt on the sixty-second floor. My palms are unexpectedly damp and I wipe them on my jeans just before the door opens in front of us. When we step out into the hallway, I place my hand on her arm, halting her. "Thank you for coming here with me. I know it's not easy to meet your boyfriend's family when we haven't been together for long, but I want them to get to know you." My hand slides down her arm to clasp her hand. "I have a little brother, Trevor. He's seventeen. He'll be here." I blurt out, nervously running a hand through my hair. "I'm sorry I didn't tell you about him before now." I pause and sigh loudly. "My dad had an affair with Trevor's mother when my parents were still married and I was four years old when he was born. Knocking his mistress up was the last straw for my mom and the end of her overlooking his indiscretions. They divorced shortly after and he's been married to Brandy, my stepmom ever since."

Harlow squeezes my hand. "It's okay. You don't need to tell me all this right now. I can figure it out for myself or we can talk about it at a more convenient time."

I quickly nod, smiling at her. "You're the best. I don't know what I did to deserve you but I'm not letting you fucking go." I pull her into my arms, holding her close.

Her arms wrap around me solidifying how happy I am she's here with me. Dropping my arms, I step back from her hold, looking her over. "Are you ready?" She nods encouragingly and I take her hand.

There are two penthouse apartments that make up the top floor. I draw her along with me to the black door that leads to the one where my family lives. Squeezing her hand, I turn the knob with my other and hold my breath as I push open the door.

Harlow gasps as we step inside and she catches sight of the panoramic view of the Midtown Manhattan skyline through the wide, high almost wall to wall windows. Smiling, I look down at her beside me. "It's an amazing view, isn't it? Every time I make it back here this view still takes me by surprise."

"It's gorgeous. I've never seen anything like it."

"Brady," my stepmom hurries over as I close the door. She hugs me tight and then holds me at an arm's distance. Her brown eyes skim over me. "I'm so glad to see you. I think you grew another inch since I last saw you."

"Brandy, I'm twenty-one, not sixteen. I think I'm done growing. Now, bulking up," I say as I curl my arm up to show off my bicep, "that's another story."

Harlow snorts next to me, reminding me I need to introduce them. "Harlow, this is Brandy." She's immediately pulled into a hug, before she gets the once over too.

"You're just a gorgeous little thing, aren't you?"

Harlow blushes adorably at the compliment. "She sure is. Is it any surprise I'd have good taste in a girlfriend?"

Brandy's eyes open comically wide. "Girlfriend?" she questions. "How long have you two been together for?"

"We met two months ago but it took me a couple weeks to charm her into going out with me."

"I think you wore me down more than charming me," Harlow interjects with a giggle.

"You have a girlfriend?" A deep voice interrupts. "How did you convince anyone to go out with you?"

I grin. "It wasn't easy, but now I've got her, I'm not letting her go." My brother walks over and we bump fists and then I pull him in for a quick hug. Glancing at Harlow beside me I introduce them. "Harlow this is my brother, Trevor. Watch out for him. He looks sweet, but he breaks hearts all over the city." My eyes swing in my brother's direction. "Don't even think of hugging her," I say as they exchange a handshake.

"Brady," Harlow says, rolling her eyes. "Way to make things awkward."

"Hey, my brother copping a feel from you would've been much worse."

"Dude, I don't need to cop a feel. I've got plenty of willing and able girls just waiting for me to crook my finger."

"Yep. He's definitely your brother," Harlow says looking between the two of us as she removes her coat. I know she's referring to his attitude and not our appearance. If it wasn't for the blue eyes we share and our height, most probably wouldn't know we were related. Trevor looks more like Brandy with his dark hair and olive skin tone. I favor my father.

"Let me take your coats," Brandy says.

"That's okay. We're going to go put our things in my room. Harlow want to see where the magic happens?" I ask raising and lowering my eyebrows at her.

She shakes her head, biting her lip to hold back a smile.

I wink at her and then turn toward Brandy. "We'll be right back." I say and then take Harlow's hand, pulling her down the long hallway running down the left side of the apartment. This is where Trevor's and my room are located. We have our own wing. My dad and Brandy's wing is on the other side of the penthouse and includes his office.

Walking into my bedroom, I breathe a sigh of relief. I've always liked this space. It would be difficult not to appreciate such an incredible view and the ample size doesn't hurt. I think I could fit all of the bedrooms from my apartment into this one.

"Here let me take that from you," I grab her coat.

"Wow," Harlow whispers as she looks out the oversized windows. "Is that Central Park?"

Dropping both our bags onto the floor, I shrug out of my jacket and throw it down on the bed along with hers. Crossing the room until I'm directly behind her, I place my chest against her back. "Yep, sure is. We'll have plenty of time to explore it while we're here." My arms slide around her waist, pulling her against me. "I'm glad you're here." I rest my chin on her shoulder and breathe in her sweet scent.

Her hands caress over mine where they rest on her stomach. "I'm glad I am too."

My hands on her hips turn her to face me. "Just so you know, the only magic that's ever happened in this room was with myself. I've never brought a girl here before." Her eyes go wide with surprise before she laughs. "What? That shocks you?" I smirk and tighten my hold on her. "Does it ruin your image of me fucking my way through the entire female population?"

"Brady," she rolls her eyes at me. "I never said I thought you were screwing everyone - just most of them," she smiles and rests her hands on my chest. My pulse races from her touch and all I want to do is see how many times I can make her come before she begs me to stop, but I don't. I take a deep breath and remind myself I need to go slow with her.

"I'm not saying I was a saint, but I think the amount of fucking around I did might've been grossly exaggerated. Now my baby brother on the other hand..." My little brother makes me look like a virgin. All he has to do is smile and all the girls come running.

"Does he play football too?"

"Yep, he's a tight end. He'll be coming to school with us next year. He's going to be a handful and I'm going to feel obligated to keep an eye on him, but it will be cool to have him playing on the same team as me. We went to different high schools since I lived with my mom full time.

"Wow, two Lincoln's at the same school and on the same team. The female student population might not be able to handle so much sexiness."

My hands leave her hips and come up to cup the back of her head, her silky hair teasing my fingers. "I'm off the market and I don't plan on letting you get rid of me. They'll only be one Lincoln for them to chase after."

"Harlow, what's your major?" my father asks from his seat at the head of the long rectangular table crafted out of zebra wood. All five of us are seated at one end of the oversized table with seven chairs going unused. They do a lot of entertaining. I'm grateful today we're the only guests. My dad turns into an asshole when there are people around to show off for or try to impress. He likes to push my buttons and ride my ass about anything to do with football.

Harlow smooths the napkin in her lap. "I'm getting a psychology degree."

"Smart choice." He nods his head. "It's a degree you can do a lot with."

She smiles tentatively. "I hope so, because I'm not sure what I want to do yet."

He chuckles. "You've plenty of time to figure it out," he says.

Is he for real?

This is the same man who's lectured me numerous times for not having every detail of my future planned out. Funny how a young, pretty face has him singing a completely different tune. He always did like the youthful ones. He met my stepmom Brandy when she was only twenty-one and he was in his mid-thirties. In his eyes, at twenty nine my mother was already past her prime. I'm surprised he's lasted this long with Brandy. One of these days she might find herself replaced with a newer model.

"Trevor, do you know what you want to major in?" Harlow asks.

He smirks, before replying and I already know this is going to be good. "I want to be a doctor."

"Wow, what a lofty goal. I'm impressed. What kind of doctor?"

"I want to be a gynecologist," he says completely deadpan.

Harlow's head turns to meet my gaze and I chuckle. I wink to let her know she can't believe anything he says. "Dude, you're so full of it. Like you'd make it through all those years of school."

Trevor laughs and gestures in Harlow's direction. "I had her going for a second there. I don't need a degree in gynecology to study pussy."

Harlow's hand moves up to cover her mouth while she keeps her eyes locked on her plate of food.

"Trevor, that's quite enough," Brandy scolds. "We have company. Please apologize to Harlow for your lack of manners."

"Sorry, I'm just playing around. I'm not sure what I'm going to major in, but I'm definitely minoring in pussy," he announces undeterred by his mother's disgust at his lack of a filter.

Harlow's head drops as she stares in her lap. I can see her teeth biting into her lip as she tries not to laugh.

Brandy narrows her eyes in his direction and looks like she wants to strangle him. "Trevor, have we taught you no manners at all? There's a guest sitting here. Think before you speak."

"Mommy," he begins, mocking what she just said. "I'm a legal adult and let's not forget about my freedom of speech rights." He winks at her and shovels a heap of mashed potatoes and gravy into his mouth.

Brandy shakes her head. "Where did we go wrong with him, Lawrence? Maybe we should've spanked him as a toddler."

"Nothing wrong with spanking." Trevor grins and wiggles his eyebrows.

Harlow snorts, then presses her lips tightly together fighting the laughter wanting to break free.

Leaning over, I press my lips to her ear. "How do you feel about spanking?" Her head snaps around to face me as I straighten up in my chair. Her cheeks are flushed a deep pink hue. She doesn't answer me. She chews on the inner edge of her bottom lip and I'd love to know what she's thinking right now.

Lowering toward her again, our eyes locked, I pause when our lips are only inches apart. I can feel her warm breath fanning over mine and it makes me want to steal her away to my room so I can taste her delicious lips right now. "I guess this is a subject we'll need to revisit at a more appropriate time."

CHAPTER FOURTEEN

HARLOW

We have the penthouse to ourselves and although I'd love to be naked and in bed with him right now, it feels amazing to just relax together on the couch. My head is in his lap while we watch his dad's ninety-inch wall mounted flat screen television. The room is wired with surround sound giving it the effect of being in our own private movie theatre. His fingers gently comb through my bangs over and over. The repetitive motion is soothing. I'm on the verge of falling asleep when his fingertips gently trace over the crescent shaped scar just below my hairline.

"How did you get this?" he asks, staring down at me.

I close my eyes for a moment, visibly swallowing before my lids raise to gaze up at him. "I was in the car with my dad the night of his accident."

"Harlow, I'm so sorry. I had no idea."

My eyes sting with the urge to cry and I glance away. "How could you? I've never told you."

"Do you mind talking about it?" he asks brushing my hair back with his fingers.

"No." I shake my head. "It was a hit and run and they never caught the guy," I explain, filling him in on all the details of what happened. His index finger traces over the scar, back and forth in a soothing manner as he listens, his eyes never leaving my face.

"I wish you hadn't gone through such difficult times. I'm sorry for your loss. I wish I'd been a part of your life back then so I could've helped you through it all."

My eyes swing up, locking with his. "You're a part of my life now." My lips curve into a small smile. His hand caresses down the side of my face, cupping my chin in his palm.

His expression is serious. "I am and I don't ever plan on that changing." His thumb drags across my bottom lip. "You're my girl. I love you."

My eyes well with tears and then overflow from his words and my heart pounds so fast it feels like it's going to take flight and leave my chest. Sitting up, I straddle his lap and rub the tip of my nose against his. His hands grip my hips as I connect our lips in a gentle kiss. Drawing back, I cup his jaw with both hands. His stubble is rough against my palms. "I love you too. So much."

"It's pretty awesome that I'm strolling around the world famous Central Park with my boyfriend, right now. I think we need a picture to commemorate this." Pulling my phone out of my pocket I hand it to Brady. "Here, your arms are longer than mine. You can be my own personal selfie stick."

He wiggles his eyebrows. "I'll be whatever kind of stick you need me to be."

Rolling my eyes at him, I snuggle into the front of his body. He wraps his free arm around my waist and takes a few pictures of us. He spins me around, handing me my phone, before he leans down to brush his cold nose against mine. Despite the icy tip of his nose, it's a mild winter day for New York City.

Slipping my phone into my pocket, I wrap my arms around his neck and pucker my mouth in an invitation for a kiss. Thankfully he's not one to miss out on an opportunity to get his lips on mine. He brushes our mouths together, teasing my top lip first and then my bottom one. Back and forth, soft as a whisper until I'm dizzy with desire.

My fingers curl into the back of his neck. "Kiss me, dammit."

He smiles only a sliver of space between our lips, before pressing into them more urgently. My mouth parts beneath his and his tongue slicks along the inside of my lower lip before biting it with his sharp teeth. "Fuck. We need to stop. You're getting me hard. I don't want to be arrested for carrying a concealed weapon in my pants."

Snorting, I whack his chest.

"Let's walk some more. There's a lot you haven't seen." We continue to wander around the park. Brady points out various features to me and entertains me with amusing stories of his youth, before the conversation takes a turn for the more serious.

"I'm sure you noticed the tension between my dad and I." He rakes a hand through his hair. "I'm not sure why, but we've butted heads for as long as I can remember. No matter what I do it's never good enough for him." He shakes his head and runs his hand over his chin. "It's like his sole purpose is to critique everything I do and tell me how it could be better."

"I'm sorry things are so strained between you guys," I offer, feeling sympathetic. I'm in a similar situation with Cindy.

"He's not like that with Trevor and I'm glad. My brother will never have to feel like he's constantly disappointing the one person he's always wanted to impress the most." He steers us to an empty park bench and we sit down. He turns to face me. "I've recently realized that I no longer worry what my father thinks and that's a huge load off my shoulders. Now, the only person I care about impressing is you. I want you to be proud of me. Your opinion is the one I value most. You're the most important person in my life, Harlow and I wouldn't want it any other way."

It feels strange to be back at school and not spending every moment with Brady. This past weekend was the best of my life. The two days we spent in New York City were a blast, but now we're back in the daily grind of school, and final exams. I miss him. At least with football season being done, I see him more than I used to. No matter how much time we spend together, I never seem to tire of him. He's an addiction I never wanted, but now that I have him, I don't want to ever be without.

Class lets out and I'm pleased with how well prepared I was for the exam. Filtering into the crowd of students in the hallway, I make my way toward the front exit. My ear buds are in and I'm silently singing along to Kings of Leon when I feel a hand grab my ass. My head snaps over my shoulder, my mouth open, ready to lay into whoever had the audacity to put their hands on me. The only person I find within groping distance is Brady and he has a giant smile on his face. His hands are up in front of him in a gesture of helplessness. "Don't hit me," he jokes.

Slowing my pace, he slides in next to me, wrapping his arm around me. I poke him in the stomach. "You're a jerk. I thought you were that Cameron dude."

Brady's steps stop, halting me at the same time. He pulls me to the side of the hallway. "Why did you think I was Cameron? Does he grab your ass?" he asks, a muscle in his cheek tensing.

I chew on my bottom lip, already regretting the words that came out of my mouth. "He grabbed my ass one night when Raine and I were out. It was before you and I were together."

He rolls his neck and clenches his fingers. "He what?" he asks, leaning toward me. His voice is deeper than I've ever heard and his expression is darker than I've ever seen.

"He grabbed my ass, but I took care of it." I place a hand on his arm, running my fingers up and down his tricep muscle. "I told him to knock it off and called him an asshole," I explain, hoping to calm him.

"I don't think your words packed the same punch my fist will."

"Brady," I pause, gripping both his arms. "I don't want you to do anything to Cameron. Please don't turn this into a big thing."

"It is a big thing. He put his hands on you." He cups my face in his large palms. "He put his hands on my girl."

"I wasn't your girl then, Brady."

He peers down into my eyes, his expression earnest, his blue eyes more serious than I've ever seen them. "You've always belonged to me; we just didn't know it yet." He places his forehead against mine and my arms wrap around his waist. My fingers burrow under the bottom of his sweatshirt and grip the soft cotton of his t-shirt while I inhale the masculine scent of his cologne.

"That was the sweetest, most romantic thing anyone's ever said to me."

He smiles, our foreheads still touching. "Bet you didn't think I had it in me."

"Nothing surprises me about you, anymore."

He straightens up, gazing down at me. "Can I surprise you with lunch? I was thinking we could grab a Gino's pizza and head back to my place for the afternoon."

Licking my lips, already anticipating the delicious taste of the pizza, I enthusiastically nod my head.

Thirty minutes later, we're kicking back on his sofa, happily holding a slice of pizza in one hand and a beer in the other - *it's five o'clock somewhere.* At least that's what I keep telling myself.

"I've never drunk during the daytime hours before. Does this mean I'm developing a drinking problem?" I ask Brady before I drink down another large sip of the beer.

He chuckles. "You're the last person who has to worry about that. I think I've seen you drink a total of three times."

"How did your exams go?" I ask winding the extra cheese around my finger and then tugging it off with my teeth.

"I think it went okay." He shrugs.

"I bet if you didn't have a football scholarship you'd be more concerned."

"You might be right, but I do have it," he says tickling my side. I squirm to escape his fingers, giggling.

"Stop, I'm going to choke on my pizza," I sputter. His fingers leave my side and I sigh in relief.

"When are we having dinner with your stepmom?" he asks out of the blue.

"I've told you like three times now, Brady. Are you messing with me?" I huff.

"Yep. I like to see you get all worked up, kitten. Your cheeks get flushed like when I make you come."

"Brady," I shout. "I can't believe you just said that to me."

"Did you decide what you're doing for the winter break?" he questions.

"I'm going home."

"And?"

"And then I'm coming back here to spend the last two weeks with you."

He leans over and brushes his lips against mine. "I'm glad you decided to come back early." He runs his index finger down my nose and then steals the piece of crust from my hand without me noticing until I watch him push it into his mouth. "Hey, that's my favorite part. You're a thief."

He winks, chewing at the same time and then takes a large gulp of his beer to wash it all down. "I was only thinking of your safety."

Raising a brow at him, I ask, "What are you talking about? I've been eating pizza for years now."

He turns to face me his shoulder leaning against the back of the couch. His hands grip my hips, pulling me toward him. I end up flat on my back, the cushions soft under me as his fingers dig into my sides. I shriek and kick, trying to wiggle away from the savage tickling, but I can't escape.

"Brady - stop. I - can't – take - anymore," I choke out.

His fingers begin to slow down, switching from tickling on top of my shirt, to caressing my skin underneath it. His eyes gleam mischievously as he hovers over me. "It's time for dessert."

CHAPTER FIFTEEN

BRADY

Pausing in front of the door, I run a hand through my hair. Shifting the bouquet of flowers and bottle of wine into one arm, I take a breath. This is the house Harlow grew up in and it's time to meet her stepmom. I'm not sure what to think of her. What I've heard doesn't paint her in a favorable light, but Harlow hasn't really told me too many details about her. I get the impression they're not close. I'm hoping to know more after dinner tonight.

I knock and it's only a few seconds before the door swings open. A breathless Harlow answers with a large smile. Her eyes shine brightly with excitement and I hope I have something to do with how happy she seems. "Hey," she squeals and throws her arms around me. *Yep, I do.* Wrapping an arm around her, I do my best to avoid crushing the flowers and dropping the wine.

"Hi. It's so good to see you." I squeeze her tight, placing a kiss on top of her head. "I missed you." We haven't seen each other for two weeks now and have only talked on the phone. I'm not a fan of phone calls, but I've learned to make an exception for Harlow. I needed to hear her voice as much as she wanted to hear mine.

I went to New York for a week and then to my mom's for Christmas. We both agreed I'd come here for dinner tonight and then Harlow will return to Boston with me. Tomorrow is New Year's Eve.

I'm looking forward to two weeks of uninterrupted time with her. My roommates are all spending the rest of the school break with their families so we'll have the whole apartment to ourselves.

"Give me those lips, kitten. I've been too long without them," I growl, my face against her neck. She tips her face up and my hand grips the back of her hair tugging her head back. Her eyes flare with surprise and then desire as my lips move closer. The first contact is whisper soft. My mouth moves over hers, barely making contact, teasing us both. Her warm breath fans over my lips in a soft sigh and all thought of teasing her is gone. Pressing my lips to hers, my tongue tastes her plump bottom lip before diving inside to become reacquainted with hers. She moans into my mouth and leans every inch of her tight body into me.

Our kiss quickly grows heated and my body responds to her touch. I want to fuck her hard against the front door, the rest of the world be damned. I want to - but I can't. Tearing my mouth from hers, I rest my forehead on hers and wait for my breathing to slow.

"To be continued later," I say with a chuckle.

Her hand slips between us and she grips my cock through my jeans. "Are you sure?"

I groan and briefly enjoy the pleasurable sensation of her fingers roaming up and down my hard length, before I pull her hand away.

"You need to behave, kitten. I want nothing more than to slam you into this door and take you hard and fast, but now is not the time."

Her eyes gleam with desire and it's all I can do to keep myself in control. I clench my teeth together and glance away from the temptation she presents with her shiny lips and the tight white sweater she's wearing.

Releasing her from my hold, I take a step backward. I need some space between us. It's been too long since we were together and I missed her even more than I expected. "Let's get inside so I can get you back to my place sooner." I wink.

"I like the way you think." She winks back and I grin at how adorable she is. She spins around and I follow her inside. My eyes scan the open entryway of the typical New England Colonial style home, while she pushes the door closed. There's a tall stairway almost directly in front of us and a railing running across the second-floor balcony.

"Here, give me your coat," she says holding out her hand. Maneuvering the wine and flowers I'm holding, I manage to shrug it off. She hangs it in a closet near the front door. Taking me by the hand, she says, "Cindy is in the kitchen preparing dinner."

I can hear the sounds of her cooking and the delicious aroma has my mouth watering. The water from the faucet is running. The clanging of pots and the sound of dishes being put away, all register in my ears as we're only a few steps from the doorway.

My stomach feels a little unsettled and I'm not sure why. I've never worried about making a good impression on someone when I meet them, but I've never been in love before. I've never had a reason to care until now which changes everything. I run a hand through my hair and glance down at my black untucked button down shirt. This is as good as it's going to get. Hopefully, she'll think I'm a good fit for Harlow.

The kitchen is large and brightly lit with maple cabinets running the length of the room up to a large sliding glass door. Harlow's stepmom is at the sink with her back to us.

"Brady's here," Harlow announces over the sound of water running. We stop about five feet from her and wait for her to finish what she's doing. She wipes her hands on a dish towel before turning around. "I'm Cindy," she says.

My eyes scan over her taking in her deep red hair and the bright pink of her lips. My heart feels like it stops and then pounds against my chest when I see the rest of her face. My throat feels like I've swallowed a boulder. *No, this can't be fucking happening.*

Her face briefly registers shock and then moves to a smile as she walks toward me.

No. No. No. I shout inside my head with every step she takes, moving closer. She holds her hand out and I don't want to touch her, but I know it's inevitable. When our skin touches, she smirks and I feel nauseous. I know my whole world is about to implode in the worst fucking way possible.

"Brady, huh? We never exchanged names that night, did we?" The scent of her floral perfume dredges up unwanted memories. My stomach clenches and rolls. I feel sick.

I don't say anything. All I can think of is the hurt this is going to cause Harlow.

"Come on, don't be shy now, sugar," she says.

"Do you guys know each other?" Harlow asks, glancing back and forth between Cindy and me.

I remain silent. I can't get past the lump in my throat to find the words to answer.

"Oh you could say that," she replies looking like the cat who just ate the canary.

"I don't understand," Harlow frowns, tucking her hair behind an ear.

Cindy opens her mouth to answer and I interrupt. "Can I talk to you for a minute?" I gesture with my head that I want to leave the kitchen.

She nervously chews on her bottom lip. "Sure. We'll be back in a few minutes," she calls over her shoulder as I tug her along with me. Once we reach the entryway, I stop and turn to face her. Taking a deep breath, I study the way her hand fits in mine.

Please don't let this be the last time I'm ever this close to her.

"I need to tell you something and you might hate me after you hear it."

She shakes her head. "I won't. Just tell me."

"I had sex with your stepmother," I blurt out, ripping the band aid clear off.

She gasps, dropping my hand and rubbing her palm along her thigh as if it burned her. "No," she whispers.

"I didn't know who she was," I quickly spit out. "I met her at a bar and we went back to her hotel room. We…"

"Stop," she shouts interrupting my hurtful words. Her eyes are tear filled. "I don't want the play by play. When did this happen? Were we together?" Her voice cracks and her hand covers her mouth as the tears begin to fall.

I grip her upper arms and stare down into her sad gray eyes. "No, it was before school started. It was meaningless. We didn't even exchange names."

"Well that makes it all better," she says, sarcasm dripping from her tone.

"I know it doesn't make it better." I shake my head. "I know nothing I can say will make this any easier for you. All I can say is I'm sorry. I wish I had made better decisions before I met you."

"I don't want to talk about this anymore." She takes a step back, breaking my hold on her. "I think it would be best if you left now."

"Harlow, no. I…" My words freeze in my throat when I take in her stricken expression. Nothing I can say at this point will matter. She needs time to process what she just learned and come to grips with the horrible truth. *If that's even a possibility.*

This might be the last time we speak. "I love you," I grit out. My teeth clenching to keep from losing my shit. I want to punch a hole in the fucking wall.

She shakes her head, tears running down her pink cheeks before whirling around. Running up the stairs, she disappears from my sight.

I resist the urge to follow her. Instead, I grab my jacket, not bothering to put it on and as my hand closes around the metal doorknob I hear Cindy's voice.

"I've thought about you often since our night together." She moves up close to my side. I stare straight at the door.

"Did you ever think about me?" Her fingers seek my arm, tracing along my bicep.

I shrug her hand off and turn my head in her direction. I'm going to make my answer crystal clear so there's no chance of her getting the wrong impression.

"No. I never thought of you again. You were just a meaningless fuck and the minute I walked out the door you were forgotten. I never thought about you again until you approached me outside of the lecture hall a few weeks ago. I was only being polite when you came over and hugged me. I'm in love with your daughter. She's the only woman I want - the only woman worth remembering."

My hand turns the knob and I slip outside. I breathe a sigh of relief as I pull the door closed behind me putting some space between me and the biggest mistake of my life. I head to my truck, but then veer off toward the garage when I catch sight of the trash barrel. Flipping open the cover, I drop the flowers and bottle of wine inside and then slam the top shut. I don't want any physical reminders of this night. The ache in my chest is reminder enough.

CHAPTER SIXTEEN

HARLOW

After throwing myself on my bed, I break into gut wrenching sobs.

How can this be happening?

When did they even meet?

My mind rolls back to the end of August. That was the last time my mother stayed at a hotel in Boston. She helped me move my stuff into my dorm and she stayed overnight to take care of some business in the city the next day. I can't believe when she left my dorm she met Brady in a bar. With all the fucking places to go out in Boston, they just had to pick the same one. If only I had asked her to stay longer or if I'd gone with her back to her hotel, then they never would've met and none of this would have happened.

But it did happen.

And I can't undo it.

Oh God.

I can't believe Brady had sex with Cindy.

What does this mean for us?

My phone started ringing only minutes after Brady left. He keeps calling, but I'm not ready to answer. I can't talk to him. Speaking with him would make all of this more real than it already is and I don't think I can handle anything else piled onto what I'm already dealing with.

Reaching over, I shut my phone off and cry until I'm so exhausted I can't keep my eyelids from dropping shut any longer.

As if I'm not dealing with enough already, I wake to stiff cheeks from all the tears I shed and swollen eyes. I wish I hadn't woken up yet. I'm not ready to think about everything that happened last night. It's all too painful and the whole situation disgusts me. I'm pissed at Brady for being such a fucking pig. Why couldn't he keep it in his pants?

And my stepmother - what the hell was she thinking? Does she make a habit of fucking strangers? Or was Brady lucky number one?

Snapping my eyes shut, I work to clear my mind. I just want to lie here and forget about everything, but it's not working. My brain is working overtime thinking about one hundred possible scenarios involving Cindy and Brady. Flashes of them in bed together keep assaulting my mind and the more I try to shut the images down, the faster they appear.

Morbid curiosity has me wondering what exactly happened between them.

Did he go down on her?

Did she give him head?

I clench my teeth and tightly squeeze my eyes shut. I don't want to be wondering these things. I don't want to think about whether he got her off or if he spent the night with her.

Shrieking with frustration, I flip the covers back, climbing out of bed. I need to get busy doing something and keep my mind occupied.

I throw on the first pair of jeans and shirt I find, then add some socks and my converse. Quickly running a brush through my hair, I secure it in a ponytail and brush my teeth. Grabbing a hoodie from my desk chair, I frown when I realize it's Brady's. Bringing the soft worn fabric to my face, I inhale his scent. Dammit. All I want to do is go to him so he can tell me it was nothing. Tell me none of this happened. It was all a bad dream. Shaking my head, I throw his sweatshirt on the floor in the corner where I won't have to look at it and choose a pink fleece jacket I've always liked. I grab my phone and my purse and I'm ready to hit the road.

When I reach the bottom of the stairs, Cindy calls out for me. I freeze in place, groaning. I don't want to face her right now.

"Harlow," she says as she walks toward me.

Too late.

Dammit, I was really hoping to avoid this.

"I wanted to talk to you and explain what happened with Brady and me."

Oh God no. I don't want to hear this. Being around Cindy is not the answer any more than seeing Brady right now would be. *Let me outta here.*

I stare at her, remaining silent and strong. I know if I open my mouth a deluge of anger with fly out of me, and an endless river of tears.

"I'm a little embarrassed you found out about us." She giggles.

She fucking giggled like a schoolgirl. She doesn't seem too embarrassed to me or slightly remorseful. I cross my arms over my chest and stare at her with no visible expression on my face.

"We had such a fabulous time that night. It's a shame we never exchanged numbers. I'm sure he's regretted it since." She clasps her hands in front of her. "We could've been together all this time and you would have been spared all this heartache." She gestures at me and shakes her head. "We did bump into each other a couple weeks ago and he was more than happy to see me. In fact, I was hoping to rekindle the flame between us - if you know what I mean." She rubs her hand over my shoulder. "This is probably for the best. Boys like him don't go for girls like you. It never works out."

"Thanks, Cindy. You're always thinking about what's best for me," I sarcastically reply.

"I know, I really do. You're the most important thing to me, Harlow."

My eyebrows raise in surprise at her words. "Which is why I think you need to stay far away from Brady. You don't need a man like him. He's the type who'd never be faithful to you. He's probably been sleeping with other girls this whole time."

Does she know something I don't? Do they plan to meet up sometime?

"He's gorgeous and guys like him love to play the field. They don't settle down until they've had their fair share of ladies which doesn't happen until they're usually well into their thirties."

Her words continue to play on my insecurities and I begin to question if any of our relationship was real.

What if she's right? Maybe he's been screwing around behind my back this whole time.

Her words echo through my mind as I hurry to the door. The walls are closing in on me and I need to get the hell away from Cindy.

"Where are you going?" she shouts. I slam the door behind me, shutting her inside, ending her hurtful words. I fumble in my purse for the keys to my white Jetta. Once they're in hand I unlock the doors and sit behind the wheel. A sob escapes me when I rest my head back on the seat for a moment and think about where I want to go. *Raine.* I need my friend and I need her asap.

Picking up my cellphone, I type out a message to her.

Me - *I hope you're home. I'm on my way.*

Raine - *I'll get the tissues ready.*

I smile as I read her reply. She knows me so well.

The drive to Raine's house takes me about ninety minutes. She lives in an affluent suburb on the north shore of Massachusetts. I'm not out of my seat belt before she's running down the front steps toward me. When I step outside the car she crashes into me, knocking me off balance and then squeezing me tight. Our hug is like the perfect metaphor for our friendship. Raine shakes my world up a little, challenging me and then she's my rock when I need her to be - holding me steady.

"I missed you. Are you okay?" She draws back to study my face.

"I missed you too. I'm not sure if I'm okay," I answer, lifting my shoulders in a shrug.

She grabs my hand. "Let's get out of the cold. There's fresh hot chocolate and chocolate chip cookies waiting inside"

"Come on," she says, leading me to the kitchen. The sweet scent of fresh baked cookies is strong in the air and my stomach growls. "Sit down." She gestures to the stools lined up under the long granite island. Pulling one out, I straddle the leather cushion and rest my feet on the stainless-steel rung around the bottom.

She gets busy plating cookies and pouring hot chocolate. Once it's all on the counter she takes the stool next to me. "So, fill me in on what's going on." She blows on her hot chocolate, studying me, before taking a sip.

"Brady and Cindy slept together."

"What?" Raine gasps, her eyes opening wide. "When?"

"It happened the night we moved into the dorm. He picked her up at a bar and went back to her hotel room. He says he didn't even get her name and it meant nothing."

Raine pushes her mug away and takes me in her arms. Immediately, sobs wrack my body and I cling to her like a lifeline. And right now, that's exactly what she is for me.

She lets me get it all out before she begins to ask questions. "Where did you and Brady leave things?"

"I told him to go; I didn't want to talk about it anymore." I sniff and wipe the tears from under my eyes.

Raine stands, walking over to open one of the cabinets. She returns with a bottle of Bailey's in her hand. "I think we need something stronger than just hot chocolate, right now," she says, pouring a considerable amount of the liquor into our mugs.

"Harlow, you're going to have to speak to him at some point. Unless you're willing to throw away your relationship over this." She soothingly rubs her hand across my back.

"I know. I keep seeing images of them together in my mind. It's horrible and I can't make it stop. I don't want to think about what they did," I sob. "It hurts too much."

"Harlow," Raine pauses until she has my full attention. "Do you love him?"

"Yes." My voice is a shaky whisper. Despite what happened with Brady and Cindy, it doesn't change my feelings for him. "I love him so much, Raine. That's why it hurts so bad."

Raine presses her lips together, studying me. "Well, you guys will need to work things out."

"I'm not convinced. Cindy said…"

"What did that bitch say now?" Raine cuts me off.

Glancing down I focus on the table. "She said guys like Brady are incapable of being faithful and he won't settle down. What if," I struggle to swallow past the lump in my throat, "what if he's been screwing around with her the entire time we've been together? What if Cindy is right and I'm not special to him? Maybe I'm just another notch on his bedpost."

"Can I say how much I've always hated Cindy? She's so busy being miserable she doesn't want you to be happy." Raine shakes her head.

"I don't know if I can ever see him as more than a player now. What happened was a giant reminder of who he is and why a girl like me should keep my distance. I just don't know how to get past the reality of him sleeping with Cindy. I can't see a way around it."

Raine leans over and hugs me so tight I can barely breathe. "Have some faith and trust you'll find a way. Listen to your heart and stop overthinking everything."

I smile for the first time in over twenty-four hours. I'm not sure what's going to happen with Brady, but I know Raine will help me get through it no matter what the outcome is.

"Come on. Let's eat some junk food and watch some television."

Ten Days Later

Returning to my dorm, the weekend before classes resume, filled me with mixed emotions. I spent the last ten days staying with Raine at her house. I couldn't bear to return to Cindy's and watch her gloat or worse hear more about how wrong Brady is for me. Raine kept me busy and my mind occupied as much as possible.

Now, I'm glad to be back at school. I enjoy learning and working hard makes me feel fulfilled, but being back here reminds me of Brady. Every corner I turn, each door I open, has my breath halting fearful I'll encounter him on the other side. It's been eleven days since I've seen him - eleven days of multiple text messages and ignored phone calls from Brady. I'm not ready to talk to him and I'm still not gaining any clarity on how I should handle this situation we've found ourselves in. I'm taking it as a sign I need more time. *What else can I do?*

"You're going to get drunk tonight," Raine informs me with a mischievous smile as we walk into the dimly lit C's Pub.

"I am? Why would I want to do that?"

"Because it will take your mind off everything and you deserve some fun."

My expression is skeptical. I remember my last drunken night. I woke up in Brady's bed the next morning. Hopefully, this night goes better.

Raine orders six shots of whiskey. She's not playing around. Shrugging, I grab one from the bar and raise it to my lips.

"Hey, not so fast. Where's our toast?" Raine asks.

I'm not really in the mood to think of anything, but one glance at her hopeful gaze and I know I can't let her down. "May we never regret this." I touch my glass to hers and down the cool liquid.

"Just for the record, getting drunk isn't any fun unless you regret it. You can do better with your next one. Maybe something a little more upbeat and less depressing." She nudges my side with her arm.

Smiling, I lift another glass from the bar. Pressing my lips together, I focus on coming up with something more appropriate. "To you and me as long as we are able to lift our glasses from the table.

"Hell yeah," Raine says, clinking her glass gently against mine. We both tip the shots back. The amber liquor burns my throat, but I like the way it's making the rest of my body feel. I'm warm all over and relaxed for the first time in almost two weeks. Now, I finally get the draw of numbing the pain with alcohol. Don't get me wrong, I haven't any plans to make this a habit, but for tonight I'm going to make the most of it.

My head snaps to the side when a large male arm unexpectedly slides around my waist. Nick is standing next to me, beaming down at me. His smile is so welcoming, I spin toward him and throw my arms around him.

"Hey stranger," he says, his lips close to my ear. "How are you?" He squeezes me as if he knows how horrible I've been. I'm tempted to stay right here, my cheek pressed against his thick chest, his arms wrapped tight around me. It's the closest thing to being in Brady's arms. I pull away and stand in front of him, letting my arms fall to my sides. I know it's not fair to use Nick as a substitute. He's a great guy, but he's not the one whose arms I'm craving with a need so powerful it's painful.

"I'm hanging in there. How was your break?" I ask, changing the subject.

"It was okay. I came back here a week ago. My boy needed me." He peers at me waiting for a reaction, but I'm not going to give him one. "How come you're not answering his texts and calls?" He hits me with the hard question I was hoping to avoid.

I shake my head. "I don't know, Nick. I'm not sure how I feel about everything. I'm still trying to work it all out." Closing my eyes for a moment, I run my fingers over my forehead to soothe the ache already beginning. Whether it's from the whiskey or thinking about Brady, I'm not sure. "For now, it's easier to leave it alone. If he can't understand how big of a deal this is for me, then that's too bad." My shoulders rise and fall in a shrug. "I'll reach out when I know what I want to say. Until then, there doesn't seem to be much point." Glancing up at him, I catch him looking over my shoulder. Turning my head to see who's there, my mouth drops open when my eyes lock with Brady's. I'm trapped by a plethora of emotions as we stare at each other. His blues convey his sorrow about what happened and his love for me. I can see it all clear as day. The way he's standing is so uncharacteristically Brady. His shoulders are slumped forward as he stands alone, leaning against the wall.

I'm disappointed in him for sleeping with Cindy and I know that's not necessarily fair, but knowing firsthand he's suffering makes me feel somewhat better. I'm glad he's as affected as I am. No matter how many times I tell myself I don't need him and we weren't together long, I know it's not the truth. Seeing him helps me to realize how much I've missed him and how much I do love him. It doesn't change the outcome though.

I swing around to face Nick. "Great. Just fucking great." I grab the one remaining shot from the bar and knock it back, noticing Raine already drank hers too. Where is Raine? I realize I've lost track of her. I must be more distracted than I realized. She's not anywhere in sight, but I know she can't be too far. Her phone is in my back pocket and she wouldn't leave without it.

"Why don't you go back to your friend?" I spit out in Nick's direction as I lean my arms on the bar.

He steps closer, his hand on my back. "Hey, you're my friend now too. This is hard on both of you." His hand rubs back and forth between my shoulder blades. "I just want you guys to work this out. Even though I think you're going to realize you belong with me." He chuckles, winking at me when our eyes meet.

I snort and flag down the bartender. I'm ready to numb all the hurt seeing Brady has dredged up.

"Harlow." His deep voice has me squeezing my eyes shut. *No.* I freeze in place, stiff as a board and pray he doesn't touch me. My eyes are glassy with tears when I open them.

"Harlow, we need to talk. Please talk to me. I miss you. I love…"

I spin around so fast he stops speaking. "Don't. Don't say another word." My eyes flash anger at him. "I'm not ready to talk to you. I want to be - but I'm not." I ignore the tear trailing down my cheek. "I know it's illogical for me to be angry about something you did before you met me, but it's not something I can push out of my mind." My arms wave madly. "I can't snap my fingers and make it go away. I need time and I'm hoping you care enough about me to honor my request."

His blue eyes beg me for forgiveness as he stares down at me. "Of course I care about you. I love you."

Holding my hand up, I stop him from saying anything else and walk away in search of Raine. I can't handle anymore tonight. Her plan to get me drunk is an epic fail and now I just want to go home.

Our dorm room is dark as I lie here, my thoughts racing around in my head. Seeing Brady tonight was difficult for me. As much as I wanted to dive into his arms and forgive him there's a part of me holding back. It's not just that he slept with Cindy. I can't help but wonder if there's more to the story than them being together one time. What if he's been sleeping with her all along? Or maybe someone else. What if he's incapable of being faithful and he can't admit it? What guy cheats and admits he has?

"Harlow," Raine pauses until she has my full attention. "I asked you this question ten days ago and I'm going to ask you again. Do you love him?"

"Yes," I whisper. "I think no matter what happens, I always will."

Raine smiles. "Well, there's your answer."

"What are you talking about?" I ask, confused.

"You love him and he loves you. That's what it comes down to. I'm sure you guys can work this out. It won't be simple and it will take some time, but it's worth it."

"I wish it were that easy, Raine."

"Brady is crazy about you. I'm not saying what happened isn't fucked up, but it did happen before he knew you. All I need to do is watch how he looks at you to know how much he cares. I don't believe for a moment he's screwing around on you."

"I want to believe he loves me as much as he says he does. I need him to be as broken up over our split as I am. At least then I'd know for sure I meant something to him."

"Aren't we friends?" Raine asks, drawing me out of my inner pity party.

"You know you're my best friend. Why are you asking me this?"

"Do you trust my opinion?" she questions.

"Of course."

"Then what makes you think I'd encourage you to forgive him and work things out unless I believed in what a good guy he is? Do you think I'd deliberately push you into a situation knowing you'd get hurt?" Her voice rings with indignation.

"No, never."

"Then trust me when I say he cares deeply for you."

I want to believe what Raine's saying. I need to believe when Brady said he loved me, he meant it.

CHAPTER SEVENTEEN

BRADY

Today's day eighteen without Harlow and it's not getting any easier. I'm at a loss. *What I should do?*

I promised her space and I've kept my word. I even stopped texting her after I saw her at the bar, thinking absence might be the best way to go. That idiotic theory fucking backfired in my face. She hasn't reached out to me once. I've been lurking around the places I know she goes on campus and every time I've seen her this past week she's turned her head the other way. If we don't talk soon, I'm worried we're going to reach the point of no return. I can't lose this girl. She's the most important person in my life. I've barely made it through the past couple weeks without her. I don't know what I should do to get her back, but I'm going to figure something out soon. I can't take much more of this painful ache in my chest. I never realized it was possible to miss someone this much.

Nick and Zeke have both been on my case. They say I've been acting like a lovesick pussy. I don't disagree with them, but I'm not going to give them any more ammo to use against me.

In an effort to prove them wrong I'm currently standing in C's pub downing shots in between beers. I've even been conversing. Although, the scowl that appears on my face so easily these days has been harder to control. I don't have the energy to pretend I'm interested in hearing about what happened at the frat party last night. I've changed so much in the last few months and it's all because of Harlow. She showed me there are more important things than partying and being popular.

My eyes move over the crowd as I listen to the endless conversations around me droning on and on. I can't wait to get out of here. I'd rather be at home, relaxing on my couch with the remote in one hand and a cold beer clasped in the other. Lifting the bottle to my lips I take a sip and my gaze wanders toward the entrance. Harlow walks in with Raine, the two of them progressing in my direction. I remind myself I was here first and resist the urge to give her space.

She's about ten steps away when she notices me. She hesitates for a second, but recovers fast as she keeps up with Raine. I study her, watching every move she makes. My eyes can't get enough of her. I'm stocking up for however long it will be before I see her again.

She touches Raine's arm, leaning in close to talk and then she heads toward the back of the bar. I watch her until she disappears from my sight and drink back the rest of my beer. I want to talk to her. I know I shouldn't, but she's not giving me much choice. Slamming the empty bottle down on the bar, my feet begin to move before it even registers in my mind. I need to clear the air and this might be my only opportunity.

It takes me a minute or two to get through the crowd and to the back hallway where the restrooms are located. When I do, I see fucking red. Cameron is caging Harlow in, back against the wall and both her hands clasped in one of his above her head.

Her eyes are wide with fear. "Let me go," she yells, her voice laced with panic. She struggles but he tightens his grip and shoves a finger in her face.

"Shut up," he yells. Enough is enough. I'm all done with this guy.

I can't control my anger and take two quick steps as if I'm exploding off the line of scrimmage at the snap of the ball. My adrenaline is racing and my heart is pumping double-time. I raise my elbow up, prepared for contact. Harlow sees me coming - Cameron doesn't.

She turns her head to the side, closing her eyes as I run straight through him, blindsiding him with a forearm shiver to the temple. The extreme force of the impact knocks him horizontal and out of his loosely laced shoes, sending him head first into the back wall ten feet away.

I stand over him, my chest puffing from my accelerated breathing and the adrenaline racing through me. Listening to him mumble incoherently, I watch as the blood starts to flow from the top of his head where it slammed into the wall. "Don't stand on the tracks when the train is coming through, motherfucker."

After a few seconds, I've settled down and regained control of my anger. Turning around I walk away, leaving him on the floor and make my way over to Harlow. I grasp her hand, pulling her along behind me as I head for the back exit. Slamming through the door, I pull her outside. We're alone in the alley behind C's. Harlow catapults herself against my chest, arms wrapping tight around my waist.

I cup the back of her head with one hand and rub her back with the other. "Are you okay?"

She nods and mumbles "yes," against my chest.

"When I saw his hands on you, I lost it." Shaking my head, I think about what a piece of shit he really is. "He'll never bother you again."

She leans her chin on my chest and stares up, locking eyes with me. Hers are shiny with unshed tears and gratitude. "Thank you. I don't know what he would have done if you hadn't found us." She shudders.

Leaning down, I kiss her forehead. "It's over now. He won't touch you again." Our eyes lock and I'm lost in the cloudy depths of gray. "I miss you so much, Harlow."

"I miss you too. I still love you," she whispers.

"What did you say?" I ask.

"I still love you." Her voice is louder and more confident this time.

I cup her cheeks in my palms. "I love you, Harlow. I always will. Do you think we can get past everything and move forward?"

She nods her head. "I want to."

"Can I take you back to my place so we can spend some time together?"

"Please. I don't want to be here any longer."

Cuddling on the couch with Harlow has me feeling like the luckiest guy in the world. She's curled into my side, an arm wrapped across my stomach while I stroke my fingers over her long soft chocolate waves. "It's so nice to have you here with me. I was afraid I'd never hold you in my arms again."

She looks up at me, her eyes shining with unshed tears. "I don't ever want to be apart from you. I was so lonely. It was horrible."

Skimming the back of my fingers down her cheek, our gazes lock. "I may never let you out of my sight again," I say with a smile. Though I'm joking, there may be some truth buried in those words. If I could be with her every minute of each day, I would be.

We settle in for some more cuddling and watch some television. We're in the middle of deciding if we should watch another show or go to bed when Zeke walks through the door with Claire.

"Hey, guys. Where's Nick?" I ask.

Claire rolls her eyes. "He ended up leaving with some redhead," Zeke says with a smirk.

Harlow and I look at each other. "I hope it wasn't Cindy," she says, giggling.

I chuckle. I had the same thought.

Standing up, I hold my hand out to Harlow. "Come on, kitten. It's been a crazy night. I'm going to tuck you in now."

She rises to her feet and I scoop her up, slinging her over my shoulder. "Brady," she shrieks. I playfully slap her ass with the palm of my hand.

"Goodnight guys," I say to Zeke and Claire as I carry Harlow off to my room.

Her skin is so soft under my fingertips as they trail up and down her arm. Lying here with her sleeping on my bare chest is the second-best thing to happen to me tonight. Harlow saying she still loves me was the first. When she said those words, I thought I was imaging it.

Warm lips lay kisses from one side of my chest to the other. I smile, keeping my eyes closed and enjoying the sensation of her soft mouth on me. Her hair teases along my skin as she moves lower, her lips now near the top of my boxer briefs.

My cock has been hard since we got into bed an hour ago, but I didn't want to start anything on our first night back together. Gripping her with an arm around her back I roll us until she's under me. "What are you doing, beautiful?"

"I was about to make you a very happy man," she says, her eyes alight with mischief.

"I'm already the happiest man in the world. I have you here in my arms where you belong." I skim a soft kiss over her brow and another on the curve of her cheek.

"Make love to me."

"You don't have to ask me twice. Being inside you is my favorite place to be." Kissing down her neck, my lips trail across her collarbone and down to wrap around one of her nipples. She moans at the contact. I slip inside her tight pussy after rolling on a condom and take my time. Keeping my strokes long and slow, each motion unhurried, I show the girl I plan on spending the rest of my life with, how much I love her. This is the way making love is meant to be. Each time is better than the last, our connection deeper than before.

My hand moves up to her shoulder, guiding her over to lay on my chest, my cock slipping from inside her. My arms wrap around her torso. "I love you so much," I whisper in her ear. "I'm never letting you go again."

"I don't plan on going anywhere. I'm sorry I made you leave and didn't try to work things out sooner," she says, a remorseful expression on her face.

"It's all in the past. Let's keep our focus aimed straight down the field toward the future."

She snorts. "Are you really comparing our relationship to a football field?"

Over the course of the next few weeks Harlow and I are inseparable for the most part. The time we spent apart made us realize how deeply we love and need each other. The two of us have fallen into a routine of spending all our time together. I walk her to all her classes, we meet up for lunch and we cook dinner together at night. I'm sure at some point we might settle in and the need to be together won't feel so urgent, but for now we have time to make up for.

Harlow's also been sleeping over each night. I love having her in my bed with me and on the rare night she's not, I toss and turn.

"Are you awake?" she asks, sitting up.

"Yeah. What's wrong, kitten?"

"Nothing's wrong. I'm about to make everything right for you."

She moves to her knees and climbs between my legs, pulling my boxers down, freeing my dick. My eyes snap open when her hand grips the base of my length and then fall closed again when she wraps her full wet lips around the tip. She slowly swallows me down. I groan and slide my fingers in her silky tresses. She moves up and down my solid cock at an agonizingly slow pace, drawing out my pleasure.

"Give me your pussy," I order. Her eyes lock with mine, my dick still buried inside her mouth. She's so fucking sexy. "Swing that fine ass of yours around and sit on my face. I want to bury my tongue inside you right now."

She releases my cock, kneeling between my legs. "Take off your shirt," I command, watching as she pulls my t-shirt over her head. She drops it to the floor. I crook my finger. "Lose the panties and give me your pussy."

She pushes them down, tugging them off, before swinging a leg over my chest and spinning around. My hands immediately grip her hips and tug her backward until her pussy lands on my mouth. She moans as my tongue sweeps through her slit and I join her when the flavor of her hits my taste buds. She's fucking delicious.

"Put your mouth on me," I growl. Flicking her clit with my tongue, my fingers dig into the skin of her ass, holding her in place. She rocks against my tongue as my cock slips between her lips. She uses her hand and her mouth together, sucking, squeezing, licking and twisting until I'm going out of my mind. I try to focus on her pleasure and fight to regain control, but she's practically wringing an orgasm out of my dick between her mouth and her fist. Tugging her clit between my lips, I gently suck on the swollen flesh while she grinds against my face. I suck harder and wiggle my tongue until she comes, calling out my name. It's the best fucking sound in the world.

She leans over, grabbing a condom from the nightstand drawer. Ripping it open and rolling it onto me in no time at all. She moves forward and guides my cock inside her hot tight pussy. We both groan as she takes me all the way to the hilt.

"Fuck yes, ride my cock, kitten. Let me see those hips move." My hands clasp her hips and help control her movements. "I've missed you so much."

Sitting up, I lay a trail of kisses across her shoulders. "I never want to be apart from you again," I whisper against her ear.

I can't take my eyes off her ass as she sensually rocks up and down my cock until my orgasm hits me quick and hard. My hips jerk beneath her and I groan as her pussy squeezes every bit of my release out of me. I'll never get enough of her.

CHAPTER EIGHTEEN

HARLOW

Four Months Later

"Surprise," I jump from the shock of about thirty people screaming at me when I walk in the door of Brady's apartment. Placing my hand on my chest, I feel my heart racing. I take a deep breath and smile at Brady as he walks toward me.

"Happy twenty-first birthday, kitten," he whispers against my lips before he connects our mouths for a spine-tingling kiss. His hand slides down over the curve of my ass earning us some wolf whistles. He pulls his mouth from mine, smiling against my lips. "Now that I'm seeing you, I'm kicking myself for inviting everyone over. You look so sexy." His lips move to the bottom of my ear, teasing along the edge. "I want you to myself," he growls.

I rub my hands over his chest. "There will be plenty of time for us to be alone."

"Where's my girl?" Nick calls out from across the room.

Brady scowls at him and I smile. Nick loves to mess with him.

"Here I am," I yell, earning a poke in the side from Brady. "Hey, that's not nice."

"Neither is saying you're his girl. I think you need twenty-one spankings to remind you who you belong to." He pulls me in front of him, wrapping his arms tight around my waist. "You're my girl and I'll fight anyone I need to for you. I'm never giving you up."

My arms circle his neck and my fingers rake through the hair on the back of his head. "I don't want anyone but you."

"Good, because you're stuck with me." His eyes stare intently at my face, carefully watching me.

"What?" I question.

"Will you move in with me? I want you with me every day."

"Are you serious?" I question.

"Completely. You had to see this coming. We spend all our time together anyway. The only thing left to do is to make it official."

"Don't ask me unless you know for sure that's what you want."

"I don't need to think about it anymore. It's what I've wanted since the first night you slept in my bed."

"When I was drunk?"

"Yep, I knew then I had to find a way to make you fall in love with me." He nuzzles my nose with his. "My diabolical plan worked. You're all mine, now."

One Month Later

"I'm coming," I shout as I hurry across the hardwood floors of our apartment. I finished moving in with Brady three weeks ago and I've never been happier. We now get to spend all our free time together.

Nick was almost as excited about me joining them as Brady was. Now he has someone to watch all his sci-fi favorites with. I've even gotten him hooked on Battlestar Galactica.

Raine found some guy who wants the second bedroom in the apartment we were set to sign the lease for. I hope she knows what she's doing. She said he's hot and she's hoping for some strings free sex as part of their roommate agreement.

I don't bother taking the time to look through the peephole, before pulling the door open as quickly as possible. I'm extremely surprised to find Cindy standing there. My mouth freezes open in an oh. Although I emailed her my new address so she could forward mail to me; I never expected her to be standing on my doorstep.

She smiles at my discomfort. "Harlow, sorry to drop by unexpectedly, but I was in the neighborhood."

"Do you want to come in?" I ask, and then kick myself for having such good manners. She doesn't deserve my kindness.

"Yes please, I need to talk to you about something."

Stepping back, I allow room for her to pass by me before I close the door. I don't ask her if she'd like a drink or if she wants to sit down. Why prolong this?

"I have something for you," she says, reaching inside her large purse. She pulls out a business size envelope addressed to me. I notice the return address is the law firm dad always used.

Taking it from her, I tear open the flap and blink repeatedly at the check I just received. *One-hundred-fifty thousand dollars*. Frozen in place, I'm numb, staring at the rectangular piece of paper made out to me and worth such an ungodly amount of money. Also enclosed is a letter explaining how my dad wanted me to turn twenty-one before I gained access to this money. I guess that explains why I didn't know of its existence until now.

"Why did you bring this to me? Why not let his attorney deliver it?

"I wanted to see your expression when you saw the check. Receiving that much money is life changing. There's nothing better than the feeling of knowing you have access to all those funds."

"I remember dad mentioning how good you'd be doing if something happened to him." I shake my head. "I never thought he'd be gone, though."

"Good thing your father had a sizeable insurance policy. I certainly earned it," she says, her lips pressed tightly together.

I inhale sharply and my eyes open wide. "Why would you say that, Cindy? You didn't love my father?"

She places her manicured hand on her chest and shakes her head. "What? Of course, I did. Why would you ask such a thing?"

"That was an odd choice of words you used." I cross my arms over my chest.

"You always did have an overactive imagination. Maybe you should be pursuing a career in writing instead of psychology." She slips her purse over the crook of her arm and jingles her keys in her hand. "I should get going. I'm glad you're doing so well. Brady's lucky that you're so forgiving and trusting." She opens her mouth to continue and I cut her off.

"Don't, Cindy." I throw my hands up in the air. "I'm all done talking with you." Stomping to the door, I open it for her.

Her high heels echo against the wood floors with each deliberate step she takes. She passes by me uttering a quick, "take care, Harlow."

"Oh, Cindy," I say, waiting for her to turn around. Our eyes meet and I allow myself to verbalize the words that are clawing their way out. "Do you ever worry?"

"About what?" she asks.

"About the horrible karma coming your way? I see a large plate of misery being served to you very soon." I take a step closer and lean toward her. "In fact, I think you've already started choking it down."

She doesn't answer me. She takes a step backward and spins around, quickly moving toward the front door of the building.

Leaning against the doorjamb, my arms crossed over my chest, I watch her until she leaves. Blowing out a large sigh, I run a hand over my forehead and down my cheek. I'm not sure what to make of the conversation we just had. What a cruel and manipulative bitch. Not only does she try to remind me of her and Brady at every turn, but she stooped low enough to make me question whether she loved my dad at all.

I have a feeling this is the last I'll be seeing of Cindy.

.

EPILOGUE

"Why am I so nervous this time?" she asks, running a hand over her ponytail.

"I don't know. You shouldn't be. No doubt she's going to love you." I smile her way and take her hand as we approach the front door of the house I grew up in. My mother had been traveling around Europe for the past six months with two of her best friends. This is the first opportunity I've had to introduce Harlow to her.

Letting us in with the key on my ring, I immediately call out for my mom to let her know we've arrived.

She comes bustling from another room with a large smile on her face. As much as I look like my father, I've always heard how I get my smile from my mom.

She holds her arms outstretched. "Honey, I'm so happy to see you."

Folding her into my arms, I kiss her cheek. "Hi, mom. It's good to see you. I brought someone I want you to meet." Pulling away from her, I grasp Harlow's hand and slide her in front of me. "This is my girlfriend, Harlow. Harlow, this is my mother."

"Mrs. Lincoln, it's so nice to meet you."

She dismissively waves her hand. "Call me Marie and give me a hug." She wraps her arms around Harlow. "I need to be on a first name basis with the girl who makes my son so happy."

Dinner conversation was full of Brady stories that had me cringing and thinking, *so this is what it's like to bring a girl home to your mother.* Listening to Harlow's laughter made all the embarrassing things my mom revealed worthwhile. After coming so close to losing her for good, I appreciate her more than ever. There's nothing I wouldn't do to make sure she's happy.

After dessert, we help my mother clear the table and load up the dishwasher.

When Harlow slips away to use the bathroom, I take the opportunity to find out what my mother thinks of her.

"How do you like Harlow?"

"I love her already. She's perfect for you," my mom says, with a twinkle in her eye.

"What do you mean she's perfect for me? I know she is, but I want to know why you're saying it."

"You guys just fit. She's not attention seeking and you are."

"Hey," I say, pretending outrage.

My mom raises her eyebrows as if to say, 'see.' "You're outgoing, she's more reserved. You guys complement each other perfectly. It's the old saying that opposites attract. They really do."

Smiling at my mom, I lean down and pull her in for a hug. "Thanks mom. I'm glad you like her because I plan on marrying her someday."

"Oh, sorry. I didn't mean to interrupt," Harlow says as she enters the kitchen.

"You're not interrupting." Glancing at my mom, I say, "I'm going to take Harlow for a walk. We'll be back soon."

"We're going for a walk?" Harlow questions, an eyebrow raised. "It's like twenty degrees outside."

I tug her against my chest, wrapping my arms around her waist. "Are you doubting my ability to keep you warm?" I run my nose up and then down the side of hers and brush my lips across her mouth.

She shakes her head then sighs when I nuzzle my lips against her neck. "Come on, I want to show you something," I say, leading her to the entryway.

"That's not the first time I've heard those words," she replies dryly.

Grinning, I hold her coat up for her while she slips her arms in each sleeve, then spin her around so I can zip the front closed. I wink at her. "It won't be the last time either." Tugging on my jacket and a cap, while Harlow pulls on the black knit hat I gave her months ago, securing it over her ears. She adds gloves and a scarf and we're good to go.

The air is crisp and bites into every inch of exposed skin. "Damn, it's fucking cold," I say and grimace.

"Is it?" she sarcastically asks.

I wrap an arm around her. "Don't worry, kitten, I'll keep you warm." I kiss the top of her head as we continue to walk down the sidewalk of the same neighborhood I used to race around on my red BMX bike.

"Where are we going?" she asks, snuggling into my side.

"You'll see." I don't want to give her any hints.

We walk for another five minutes, before we come to a narrow path leading into the woods. Following the worn ground, I keep her next to me.

"Are you taking me deep inside the woods to murder me?" she jokingly asks.

"Damn, you got me. Now what am I going to do with you?" I say. Leaning down, I growl and gently bite her neck eliciting a melodic giggle.

We reach a clearing and now it's evident we're in a small park. We pass by swings and slides and keep progressing forward until we come to a football field. The lights around the perimeter are bright and light the entire area for us. I don't stop until we're standing in the middle of the field.

I turn to face her, still holding her hand. "This is where I discovered my love for football. I played on this field as a kid and now this is one of my favorite places. I like to come here when I need to think or clear my head." I run the back of my fingers down her cheek. "I never gave you one of the birthday gifts I purchased for you." A smile teases at the corners of her lips. "I wanted to wait until I could share this place with you. I know it's just a field to most, but this place feels magical to me. It's where dreams were born - my dream of playing football - and my dream of falling in love with you." Cupping her face in both my hands, I stare down into her alluring gray eyes. "I can't count the times I've sat alone on this field and imagined what it would be like to meet a girl who was perfect for me. Someone who'd see me for who I am, and not my last name. Now that I have, I'm never going to stop showing you how much I love you."

Her bottom lip wobbles with emotion and I steady it with my thumb. I trace over the plump shape and then reaching inside my pocket, I pull out a small box wrapped in shiny silver paper. "This is for you." Holding my hand out in front of her, the gift rests on my palm.

She tentatively takes it from me and then quickly tears off the paper while I watch, chuckling at her eagerness. She shoves the tattered wrapping in her pocket and gazes up at me before her focus moves back down to the little black box. She opens the lid and her mouth drops open when she sees what's inside.

"I wanted to get you something meaningful. The football can represent time you spent with your dad and how we came together. The letters are self-explanatory."

"Brady, it's beautiful." She stares in awe at the white gold football charm suspended from a fragile chain with a capital H and B made from diamonds. "Will you put it on me?" She holds it out, pinched between her glove covered fingers.

Taking it from her, I undo the clasp, drape it around her neck and then fasten it. She turns around, a full smile on her lips as she stares down where it rests on her chest. "I love it almost as much as I love you." She steps forward, wrapping her arms around my neck and tipping her face up to meet my lowering lips.

"I love you," I whisper before sliding my cold lips from one side of her mouth to the other, kissing each corner. She presses on the back of my neck letting me know she wants more and my tongue moves inside to rub against hers. I drink her in, losing myself in the heat of our kiss. One hand grips her ponytail, tugging her head back while the fingertips of the other one gently trace over the curve of her cheek. I never want this moment to end. Kissing her for a lifetime won't be enough, but I plan on doing just that. No matter what flags life will throw in our path, and I know there will be plenty, I'll do whatever it takes to get us through and come out with a win. I want it all with Harlow and nothing will stand in my way.

THE END

ABOUT AUTHOR

Jacob Chance grew up in New England and still lives there today. He's a martial artist, a football fan, a practical joker and junk food lover.

Jacob's Books on Amazon:

QUAKE I QUIVER I DELVE I TIED I DELUDE

Aces & Eights Series by Logan Chance and Jacob Chance

RANSOM

Author Links:

Facebook
https://www.facebook.com/jchanceauthor/

Instagram
http://www.instagram.com/jchanceauthor

Amazon
https://www.amazon.com/author/jacobchance

Spoiled by Chance Reader's Group
https://www.facebook.com/groups/103288340096103/

Twitter:
https://twitter.com/JChanceAuthor

Newsletter
http://eepurl.com/cAyr6L

BookBub:
https://www.bookbub.com/authors/jacob-chance

Made in United States
Orlando, FL
23 January 2022